The Clue at Black Creek Farm

Read all the mysteries in the

NANCY DREW DIARIES

✑

Nancy Drew DIARIES™

The Clue at Black Creek Farm

#9

CAROLYN KEENE

Aladdin

NEW YORK LONDON TORONTO SYDNEY NEW DELHI

ALADDIN

An imprint of Simon & Schuster Children's Publishing Division

1230 Avenue of the Americas, New York, NY 10020

This Aladdin paperback edition May 2015

Text copyright © 2015 by Simon & Schuster, Inc.

Cover illustration copyright © 2015 by Erin McGuire

Also available in an Aladdin hardcover edition.

All rights reserved, including the right of reproduction in whole or in part in any form.

ALADDIN is a trademark of Simon & Schuster, Inc., and related logo is a registered trademark of Simon & Schuster, Inc.

NANCY DREW, NANCY DREW DIARIES, and related logo are trademarks of Simon & Schuster, Inc.

For information about special discounts for bulk purchases, please contact Simon & Schuster Special Sales at 1-866-506-1949 or business@simonandschuster.com.

The Simon & Schuster Speakers Bureau can bring authors to your live event. For more information or to book an event contact the Simon & Schuster Speakers Bureau at 1-866-248-3049 or visit our website at www.simonspeakers.com.

Cover designed by Karin Paprocki

Interior designed by Karina Granda

The text of this book was set in Adobe Caslon Pro.

Manufactured in the United States of America 0415 OFF

2 4 6 8 10 9 7 5 3 1

Library of Congress Control Number 2014952479

ISBN 978-1-4814-2940-5 (hc)

ISBN 978-1-4814-2939-9 (pbk)

ISBN 978-1-4814-2941-2 (eBook)

Contents

Dear Diary,

WHO WOULD SABOTAGE AN ORGANIC farm? Especially one that's run by someone as kind as Sam Heyworth, owner of Black Creek Farm and CSA.

That's the question I'm facing after someone became seriously ill from Sam's produce—which turned out to be crawling with deadly bacteria. Sam swears his farm is clean, and I, for one, believe him. I'm usually not one to freak out over organic fruits and veggies, but I need to figure this one out— before another person is poisoned!

CHAPTER ONE

Food for Thought

"I'M JUST *SAYING*," MY FRIEND BESS MARVIN said as we pushed open the door of the River Heights Community Center, "I don't see how you can get this excited about *vegetables*."

She was talking to George Fayne, her cousin and my other best friend, who was following behind with an expression like she'd just sucked on a lemon. Ned Nickerson, my boyfriend, was right behind George with an amused look on his face.

"They're not just *vegetables*," George said, in the frustrated tone of someone who'd been arguing with the same person nearly since birth. "They're organic, sustainable, *locally grown* vegetables. And fruits too!"

"I just think it's all a little silly," Bess said as we entered the community center gymnasium, which was set up like a banquet hall, filled with round tables covered with red tablecloths and enticing combinations of fresh harvest products. A banner welcomed us: FIRST ANNUAL BLACK CREEK FARM CSA BANQUET AND HARVEST CELEBRATION.

George glared at her cousin. "How is organic farming *silly*?" she demanded.

Ned spoke up. "I might see what Bess is getting at," he said, giving George a disarming grin. "Not that any farming is silly, but . . . you know, scientists have been trying for years to prove that organically grown produce is better for you, and they've found very little evidence."

"Well, thank you, Dr. Science," George grumbled.

I held up my hands in the gesture for truce. "All right, all right," I said.

I was saved from further arguing by the interruption

of a grinning blond woman with a purple streak in her hair.

"OMG, Bess and George!" the woman cried, appearing out of nowhere to pull the two cousins into a big hug. "You guys are so *big* now! The last time I saw you, you were kids . . . now you're *young ladies*, as my grandmother would say!"

George and Bess exchanged glances and smiled as she slowly let them go.

"Holly," George said, "we're so excited that you invited us to this!" She paused to introduce Ned and me to Holly. "Guys, this is Holly Sinclair. She was Bess's and my *awesome* Girl Scouts leader and now she's assistant manager at the community center."

Holly shook each of our hands excitedly. "I'm so happy you could come!" she said, her cheeks flushed. "Black Creek Farm CSA is doing some *really* good work, trying to change the way our food gets grown," she continued, growing serious. "They just need some more support from the community. So I convinced them to throw this dinner so people can taste their food!"

"Holly, I told you," Bess said teasingly, "I like organic farms and all, but we're not exactly the culinary decision makers in our families. And my mom *really* likes the Stop-N-Go," she added. "Especially since they put in that Starbucks."

Holly shook her head, her dark eyes shining. "Your mom probably wouldn't like it so much if she knew where all that mass-produced food was coming from, or what it's doing to the environment," she said. "Come on, guys, have a seat with me."

Holly led our small group to a nearby table, where we all pulled out chairs.

"Soooo," Holly began, sliding into a seat next to George, "you must know that the produce you buy in a grocery store isn't all from around here, right?"

"Of course," Ned said. "But that goes without saying. Not every climate will be able to produce every fruit or vegetable there's demand for."

"That's true," Holly agreed, "but do you think people really consider where their food comes from, when it's so shiny and easy to buy at the supermarket?

Maybe that orange was picked before it was ripe and flown in on a cargo jet, or else trucked around the country using tons of fossil fuels and releasing all kinds of toxins into the environment. But if people stopped and thought about eating locally, maybe they'd select an apple that was grown down the road—perfectly ripe and much easier to transport."

Ned sighed. "Right," he said.

"Local food usually tastes better too," George pointed out. "Because local farmers don't pick their produce until it's ready. Produce that's trucked in has to be picked much earlier, and that affects the flavor."

Holly smiled at her. "Exactly," she said. "And we haven't even touched on organic versus conventional produce, and how many toxins are released into the ecosystem by conventional fertilizers and pesticides."

Ned spoke up. "But scientists haven't found much of a *nutritional* difference between organic and conventionally grown food," he said.

Holly shrugged. "That's true," she said, "but we

don't have to look very hard to find the damage that conventional farming does to the environment."

Bess thought a moment. "Even if I can see the logic in what you're saying," she said, "I don't do the grocery shopping, Holly. My mom does it, and she's big on bargains."

Holly nodded slowly. "Bess, all I ask is that you listen to the presentation tonight, and if you're impressed, if you like the quality of the food we serve, you *mention* us to your mom. Or pass on some flyers I'd be happy to give you." Holly turned from Bess to look at George, Ned, and me. "That goes for all of you," she said.

I glanced from George to Ned. George was nodding enthusiastically, and even skeptical Ned gave Holly a small smile. "Fair enough," he said.

"Sure," I agreed. While I didn't always eat organic, I definitely believed in being environmentally responsible. And everything Holly had said made sense.

"Oh, look!" Holly pointed behind my head at a tall, gray-haired, and bearded man. She stood up and waved, and the man turned to her and nodded. "That's Sam Heyworth, the man of the hour."

"Who?" asked Ned.

Holly smiled. "Sam's the founder and owner of the Black Creek Organic Farm and CSA."

"So what is a CSA, exactly?" I asked. The term was familiar, but I wasn't totally sure what it meant.

Holly's eyes sparkled. "I'm *so* glad you asked! CSA stands for 'community-supported agriculture.' Do you know how a CSA works?"

I shook my head.

"It's basically a way to help keep small farms in business, and help people who live in the suburbs get access to fresh, local, in-season produce," she explained. "If your family joined, for example, Nancy, they would pay an up-front fee for the whole growing season—June through November. And every week during that season—or every other week if you bought a half share—you'd come to this community center to pick up the freshest, most in-season veggies and fruits that grew on the farm that week."

I raised my eyebrows. "Picked that *week*?" I asked. "That's pretty fresh."

Holly nodded. "Right off the farm, my friend. It's as fresh as it gets."

I glanced up to see the bearded man Holly had identified as Sam Heyworth headed our way, followed by a woman about his age with short blond hair. Holly looked up at them and smiled.

"Sam can tell you everything you want to know about the CSA," she said cheerfully. "Black Creek Farm means a lot to him, doesn't it, Sam?"

Sam walked up to the table and smiled down at Holly. "You know it does," he said, looking around at me and my friends. "Hello. Friends of Holly's, I assume?"

George's eyes twinkled. "Holly was our Girl Scouts leader," she said. "She won't stop talking about your farm and CSA."

Sam chuckled. "Well, I'm flattered," he said. "Running Black Creek Farm is a dream of mine. I gave up a partnership at my law firm to build it."

Ned raised an eyebrow. "So you were a lawyer, and now you're a farmer?" he asked.

"Right," Sam replied. "And I was a stressed-out, unhappy man, frankly, but now I'm"—he stopped and turned to look at the blond woman, who'd come to a stop beside him—"very content," he finished. "Ladies and gentlemen, allow me to introduce my wife, Abby. She's given up a lot to support me in pursuing this dream."

The woman turned to me and my friends with a warm smile, her eyes crinkling at the corners. "Hello, everyone," she said. "I hope you're hungry!"

"We're starving," Bess promised.

Abby and Sam laughed. Sam glanced up, catching the eye of a thirtysomething man with short brown hair and boxy black glasses. He raised his hand, waving the man over. The man nodded, then gestured for a very pregnant woman with long red hair to follow him.

"This is our son, Jack, and his wife, Julie," Abby explained. "They're from Chicago, but they've been visiting us while they house-hunt in the area."

"Hi," said Jack, stopping a few feet away and looking from face to face with a quizzical look.

Julie stopped right behind him. "Hi, everyone," she said. Now that she was closer, I could see that she looked a little pale. "Oh, gosh, I need to sit down."

Jack looked at her with concern. "Go have a seat!" he said urgently. "In fact, go grab something to eat in the kitchen."

"That's right, dear," Sam said. "You're eating for two, remember."

Julie shot a small smile at my friends and me. "Sorry to be rude," she said, "but I think I might take Sam up on that. I've been so hungry lately!"

"When are you due?" Bess asked warmly.

"One more month," Julie said, patting her round belly.

She waved and walked toward the kitchen. I followed her with my eyes and was surprised when I heard harsh voices coming from nearby.

". . . should've planned for her to eat first," Jack was

saying to his father, a sharp edge in his voice. "She's eight months pregnant!"

Sam looked hurt. "And nobody minds her sitting down or eating early."

"Are you *sure*?" Jack asked in a lower voice, sneering. "You don't want us out here shaking hands to sell your stupid vegetables?"

Sam's face drooped even farther. Abby shot Jack a warning look. "Now, Jack . . ."

Holly cleared her throat. She was staring straight ahead, and I couldn't tell whether she'd heard the argument and was ignoring it, or had really zoned out during the whole thing. "I *am* getting hungry, Sam," she said, looking up at him. "And the hall is filling up."

She gestured around at the other tables. I noted that she was right; while only three or four tables had people sitting at them when we'd arrived, now nearly all of them were populated. They were filled with a combination of men and women, young and old. I found myself feeling hopeful for Sam and Black Creek Farm. It was hard not to be touched by his enthusiasm.

I hoped some of these diners would become customers.

Jack shook his head and walked off in the direction of the kitchen, and Sam looked down at us with an awkward smile.

"I should go check with the kitchen," he said. "Maybe we're nearly ready to eat."

He and Abby strode off, and I looked at my friends. George was frowning at Holly.

"*That* was weird," she said.

"What?" Holly asked, crinkling her brow like she had no idea what George was referring to.

"You didn't see that?" Bess asked, her blue eyes widening in surprise. "Jack just got pretty snarky with his dad."

"Oh, Jack." Holly rolled her eyes, waving her hand like Jack wasn't worth worrying about. "He's just . . . high-strung. He gets like that with everyone."

Ned shrugged. "Maybe he was just worried about his wife," he suggested.

"How do you know Julie and Jack?" I asked Holly.

"Oh, we went to high school together," she replied.

"The two of them ended up going to the same college and then settling in Chicago after they got married. It's great having them back here in River Heights."

I smiled. "Must be nice to reconnect with old high school friends."

Holly nodded, then looked over to what I assumed was the kitchen door, where Sam was striding out. "Ooh," she said, "it looks like Sam is going to speak now. That must mean dinner's ready."

I looked toward the podium that had been set up at the front of the room. Sam strode up to it and gently tapped the mic.

"Ladies and gentlemen," he said, leaning in with a smile. "Welcome to the first annual Black Creek Farm showcase and buffet dinner! I'm so delighted that all of you could be with us tonight, and I can't wait for you to taste the produce we're growing organically and sustainably on the farm. I hope many of you will consider joining our CSA. You can grab a brochure with our membership and price info, or just come grab me later! I'd be happy to give you details."

Then his face became more serious. "Ladies and gentlemen, Black Creek Farm is a dream of mine, but it's also something I feel very passionate about. A little over a year ago, I was working as a lawyer at a high-powered firm in Chicago. I took on the case of a young man whose wife had died of salmonella poisoning. Do you know what killed her?" He paused, looking around at the crowd. "Spinach," he said finally.

"That's right—packaged, washed spinach. You know those salad mixes you see at the grocery store. All this woman had done—she was only twenty-five—was buy and eat some salad. But that salad was poisoned with salmonella, because our food system in this country is broken."

I glanced at Ned. I expected him to be wearing his detached, skeptical look, but instead he looked stunned and totally absorbed in what Sam was saying. Bess and George seemed enthralled too. And Holly was glancing around at the crowd's reaction, smiling.

As we watched, Sam went on to recount where salmonella comes from (meat), and how produce becomes tainted with salmonella (through contaminated processing equipment). I had to admit that it was shocking how easily these poisons could make their way into packaged food and how damaging they could be once they were there. But Sam went on to talk about larger problems with big corporate farms: the damage they could do to the environment, and the lack of oversight.

"Not to mention," he added, "the food doesn't taste that good. Why would you want to eat a tomato that was picked two weeks ago, barely orange? It's never going to beat a tomato that ripened in the sun on my farm."

He paused, clearing his throat. I noticed that there were tears in his eyes. *He really cares about what he's saying,* I thought.

"These are issues that affect me deeply," Sam finished. "So deeply that I gave up my six-figure income and the career I'd worked decades to build, and spent my life's savings on a little farm just half an hour from here, in Idaville." He looked up, his gaze moving from table to table. "I can promise you this," he said. "The food from my farm has been lovingly grown and is delicious and safe for your family to eat." He smiled. "I hope you all will join me on my quest to make food safer, environmentally responsible—and delicious!"

Sam stepped back from the podium, and the audience erupted into applause. I clapped loudly, glancing at Ned, and saw that he was applauding heartily too. In fact, everyone at our table seemed moved by the speech—even Bess.

When the applause died down, Sam moved back from the podium and Abby scooted in, leaning toward the mic to announce, "You'll all be happy to know that the food is ready! We're going to start lining people up to move through the buffet line along the right wall, near the kitchen. Tables one through four, would you like to head over?"

I looked at the number posted in the center of our table: four.

"That's us!" Bess said, jumping up excitedly. "And not a moment too soon! I could eat a horse."

Holly laughed. "Um, I don't think that's on the menu here, Bess. It's all vegetarian."

Bess shrugged. "Then I guess a really big eggplant will have to do."

My friends and I moved toward the line that was forming near the buffet table, as Holly ran into the kitchen to help a slim Asian girl around my age bring out dishes of food. I felt my stomach growling as I spotted something that looked like pasta pomodoro, some kind of vegetable curry, and . . .

"Oh my gosh," George whispered in a hiss, and I pulled my eyes from the buffet to follow her concerned glance.

"Ohhh. . . ."

I felt my stomach clench again, this time with concern, as I spotted Julie, Jack's pregnant wife, stumbling from the kitchen. Her face was slick with perspiration, and she grabbed the door frame to steady herself.

Holly was just coming out of the kitchen with a big basket of bread, and she looked, stunned, at Julie. "Are you okay?" she cried, putting the basket on the floor and leaning closer.

"I don't think so," Julie whispered, her words slurring. "I feel . . ."

But before she could finish her sentence, she lost her grip on the door frame and went down—tumbling to the ground and splaying on the floor.

"Oh no!" Holly cried, kneeling and turning Julie over. "*Jack!* Where are you?!"

I heard running and turned to see Jack sprinting over from a table near the edge of the room. "What's happened to her?" he yelled. "Call an ambulance!"

Holly dug into her pocket for her phone, and in the confusion, the young girl who'd been helping set up the food ran out of the kitchen and surveyed the scene, her face paling in horror. She turned toward the buffet, where people were eagerly grabbing plates and piling them with vegetables.

"DON'T EAT THE FOOD!" she cried, running over and grabbing the spoons out of people's hands. "IT'S NOT SAFE!"

~

CHAPTER TWO

Dangerous Vegetables

"NOT SAFE TO EAT?" GEORGE ASKED OUT loud, her brow furrowed. "What does that mean?"

The girl was pulling the food back, out of the reach of the people who already surrounded the buffet table.

"Julie just finished eating," she said quickly, shooting Holly a concerned look. "It seems like she's having a reaction to the food."

"Oh no," Holly whispered, her gaze going blank. But then she seemed to shake herself and ran behind the table. "Yes, EVERYONE BACK UP! We won't be serving dinner until we get this figured out."

Together, Holly and the other girl, who was wearing a handwritten name tag that read LORI, packed up the food that had been placed out and carried it back to the kitchen. The people gathered around the buffet table made little murmurs of disappointment, but most everyone's eyes were on Julie, still sprawled on the floor, now with her head in her husband's lap. He fanned her with a folded napkin, but she remained unconscious.

I looked from Julie to Ned, standing next to me. He looked as worried as I felt. "A bad vegetable can make you that sick?" he hissed to me under his breath. I shrugged; I'd been wondering the same thing.

It was only minutes before the paramedics arrived—running into the community center with a stretcher and heading right to Julie's side—though it seemed like hours. They used smelling salts to revive Julie, who blinked at them, confused.

"How are you doing?" the female paramedic, whose name tag read ERICA, asked her.

Julie frowned. "Not so good," she murmured. "I feel like—I—"

Erica seemed to read her thoughts as she raised Julie's head and turned it to the side. I heard the sounds of vomiting and glanced uncomfortably at Bess and George, who looked horrified.

"There, there," said Erica, looking back at her colleague and making a gesture that looked like a shot. "Get it out, and then we'll give you something to stop the vomiting."

The male paramedic—his name tag read JAMES—produced a small vial and injection needle. He swiftly injected the needle into the vial, sucking up the clear liquid, then pulled it out and stuck the needle into Julie's arm. "This will make you feel much better," he said, "so we can get you to the emergency room."

Jack looked like he wanted to jump out of his skin. "Will she be all right?" he demanded as the paramedics worked together to load Julie onto the stretcher. "Will the baby?"

"This looks like a pretty intense case of food

poisoning," Erica said seriously. "Since she's pregnant, we need to be careful to keep her hydrated, or it can make things difficult for the baby."

She and James strapped Julie in. "We're going to get her the best of care, sir," James said. "Once we stop the vomiting and get her hydrated, she'll feel much better."

Sam and Abby were standing close by, watching the action with concerned faces. "You said 'food poisoning,'" Sam said, a questioning look on his face.

Erica nodded. "Of course we won't know for sure until we can get her to the hospital and run some tests. But to me, this looks like salmonella, listeria, or E. coli. The effects are more intense on pregnant women."

Sam still looked confused. "But all Julie's eaten today is food from my farm," he said. "We're a small-scale, organic facility. You're telling me she got food poisoning from *my* vegetables?"

Erica looked from Sam to Julie, one eyebrow raised. "Sir, we won't know anything for sure for a few hours," she said. "But in the meantime, I wouldn't serve those vegetables to anyone else."

Sam's face fell as Erica and James worked together to hoist the stretcher into the air and carry Julie toward the door. Jack followed his wife but stopped short as he passed his father.

"This is *just* what I've been saying," he hissed, so low that I could barely make out the words. "You're a lawyer, not a farmer! And now Julie's paying the price."

He shook his head and stomped off, leaving Sam looking crestfallen. "There's nothing wrong with my vegetables," he muttered after a moment, but Jack was already out the door, helping the paramedics load Julie into the ambulance.

A murmur went through the crowd, and Holly approached Sam and Abby. I watched the three of them huddle together and whisper for a moment before Abby split off and yelled, "Attention, please!"

All eyes turned to Abby, who was shaking her head and looking disbelievingly toward the kitchen. "I'm so sorry," she said quietly, and when Holly made a *speak up!* gesture, raised her voice enough to be heard over the crowd. "We're so sorry! There seems to be some sort of misunderstanding, a concern about the safety of the food tonight. Our daughter-in-law, Julie, got quite ill after eating an early dinner."

The noise from the crowd intensified as people expressed their surprise. I could hear snatches of conversation all around me:

"... produce made her *sick*?"

"Poor girl was pregnant ..."

"... What are they *up to* on that farm?"

Abby seemed to hear the chatter too and shook her head defiantly. "I know our growing practices are safe. I hope we have the opportunity to prove that to you soon! But for now, I'm afraid ..."

Her voice trailed off. Sam, who'd been in the corner, stepped up behind her.

"The dinner is canceled," he said in a deep, matter-of-fact voice.

A blip of nervous laughter went through the crowd, followed by the dull roar of surprised conversation. I looked around at the other audience members, who were shaking their heads and walking back to their tables to collect their things.

"Guess we won't be joining *this* CSA!" I heard one middle-aged blond woman say to the man I assumed was her husband.

Nervously, I looked back at Sam. From his disappointed face, I knew he had heard the woman too.

It wasn't long before the community center had nearly emptied out. Soon my friends and I were standing alone with Sam, Abby, Holly, and Lori.

Sam was staring at the floor. Abby took his hand and squeezed it, and he looked up at her and gave a deep sigh. Then he turned to Holly and Lori.

"Holly, Lori," he said, "how did this happen?"

Holly shook her head. "It beats me," she replied, looking truly mystified. "Lori and I handled all the food prep ourselves. I personally made sure that everything was properly washed and cooked."

Lori nodded, pushing her long, dark hair behind her ears. "Everything was scrubbed and cooked, or just scrubbed. I really don't understand how there could have been *anything* on those vegetables that could make a person sick—much less salmonella or E. coli."

"Where do salmonella and E. coli come from?" I spoke up. Sam, Abby, and Holly all turned to face me, surprised, as though they'd forgotten I was there.

"They both come from animals," Sam replied, shrugging. "Which makes it very strange they were found on my vegetables. We don't have any animals on the farm except for a coop full of egg-laying chickens, and they're way over on the other side of the property from the vegetables."

I frowned. "So how could—"

But Holly spoke at the same time, throwing up her hands. "What do we do now?" she asked, looking at Sam and Abby. "This dinner was our last-ditch attempt to get new CSA members. And now it's ruined! How can we keep Black Creek Farm going?"

I saw Sam wince at the words "last-ditch."

"We just *do*," he said, "because I'm never giving up on this farm."

Abby put her hands on his shoulders. "We have to get to the bottom of this," she said. "There must be some mistake. There's no way our produce would make someone sick."

Holly shook her head. "How could this be a mistake? You all saw Julie go down."

George tapped her lip. "Well, either the salmonella or E. coli was on the vegetables in the kitchen," she pointed out, "or else someone *put* it there."

Holly turned to her former Girl Scout in surprise. "Yeesh, George," she muttered. "That's quite the conspiracy theory you've got there. And who put the E. coli on the veggies? Colonel Mustard with the infected cow bile?"

George smiled. "Maybe I am being overly suspicious," she said, "but only because I happen to hang out with the World's Best Teenage Detective!" As I tried to blend in with the carpeting, my friend turned and pointed an indigo-painted fingernail in my direction. "Nancy, can't you help them out?"

I looked up into the circle of bewildered faces and

cleared my throat. "Um, George may be overstating things. . . ."

But Bess was shaking her head wildly. "She's not at all," she insisted. "Nancy is *amazing* at catching crooks. It's like it's in her blood."

Abby glanced at Sam, tilting her head to the side in a questioning way.

Sam laughed. "Well, the World's Best Teenage Detective is someone I want on my side," he said. "Nancy, might you have the time to help us?"

I looked from George's and Bess's eager faces (*I'll get you two for this later,* I thought) to the skeptical face of Holly, to the open, hopeful faces of Sam and Abby. Seeing the farmers' expressions, I sighed. *I can't turn them down,* I thought. But also, my heart was pounding at the thought of these nice people being potentially tricked. *And if someone* is *setting them up,* I thought, *I can't let that crook get away.*

Bess had been right. The need for justice *was* in my blood.

"Okay," I said. "I'll do whatever I can."

...

An hour later Bess, George, and Lori were heading home, Holly and Abby had made their way to the hospital to check on Julie (who was now resting comfortably, per a call from Jack), and I was walking out with Sam as Ned went to get the car.

Sam's phone pinged and he pulled it out, checking a text and sighing deeply. "This is a disaster," he said. "Until we get to the bottom of what's going on with our vegetables, we have to put all sales and CSA orders on hold. That's thousands of dollars. This could sink us."

I frowned sympathetically. "That's awful. I hope Ned's friend can help us figure out what's on the vegetables." Ned's a student at River Heights University, and he'd offered to take some samples of the food Julie had eaten back to the campus with him. He had a biology major friend, Rashid, who might be able to test them for contaminants. "How do you think the E. coli, or whatever it is, is getting on your vegetables?" I asked.

"I don't know," Sam said. "That's the honest truth."

I tilted my head. "How does it normally happen? Like when there's an outbreak, and produce is recalled?"

"Well, it's usually on a big factory farm, and what they typically find is that it was transferred by contaminated farming or processing equipment," Sam explained. "You know, it gets on a tractor or a picker. Then it gets on all the veggies. But we don't use any fancy tools at Black Creek. Unless *these* count." He held up his hands.

I nodded. "Could some*one* be transferring it? Someone doesn't wash their hands before picking the vegetables, and . . ."

"It's possible, but not very likely," Sam said. "The thing is, E. coli comes from *inside a cow*. Literally, from inside their digestive system. It's not the sort of thing you might just be walking around with on your hands."

I tapped my chin, thinking. I was stumped. "Do you fertilize your crops with cow manure?" I asked.

Sam shook his head. "Nope. We only use plant-based fertilizers."

I heard something behind me and turned to find Ned pulling up in the car.

Sam glanced at Ned and held up his hand in a small wave. "Listen, we really appreciate your looking into this, Nancy. You've gone above and beyond already, staying this late, getting your boyfriend to bring the samples to his friend. Go home and get some sleep. Maybe we can talk later."

I was still thinking, trying to reason out how an animal-based virus had gotten itself onto Black Creek Farm's organic produce. "Can I come take a look at the farm?" I asked.

Sam's eyes lit up. "Of course you can!" he said happily. "I'd love to show you around. I'm proud of what we're doing there."

I smiled. "Great," I said. "I'll call you and set up a time." I reached into my pocket and fingered the business card Sam had given me earlier. BLACK CREEK FARM—WE RAISE HAPPY FRUITS AND VEGETABLES!

Sam reached out and clasped my shoulder. "Thank you, Nancy," he said passionately. "I can't tell you how much this means to me. This farm, this CSA—it's my dream." He paused, clearing his throat. "And this is my last chance to save it."

I gently put my hand on top of his. "I'll do everything I can," I said. "You have my word. If someone is sabotaging Black Creek Farm, we'll get to the bottom of it."

~

CHAPTER THREE

Occam's Razor

NED RAISED HIS HANDS TO HIS FACE, pretending to blush as he opened the door to his dorm room to find me.

"Oh, gosh!" he said. "A visit from my always-busy girlfriend. Did you come to help me study for midterms? Maybe you brought me some chocolate-chip cookies to fuel my late nights?" He batted his eyelashes goofily.

I shoved him. "You know why I'm here," I chided. "And sadly, no, I didn't bake any chocolate-chip cookies."

Ned made a horrified face. "I didn't mean you had *baked* them," he teased. "I wouldn't want you to burn your house down. I meant maybe you'd brought over some that *Hannah* made."

I groaned. "Just for that, I'm not giving you these oatmeal raisin cookies from Hannah! I'm going to eat them all myself!" I held up the plastic bag containing five cookies, which my dad's and my longtime house-keeper and cook had *insisted* I bring over to Ned. Hannah was famous (in River Heights, at least) for her oatmeal raisin cookies. She'd once tried to teach me how to make them, and yes, I admit, there had been fire involved.

Ned grabbed the cookies out of my hand and ran over to his desk, tearing the bag open and devouring one. "Uhhhmmmm," he moaned through a mouthful of crumbs. "Why only five?"

I smiled. "Because Hannah said she knew you'd be sitting around studying all day," I replied. "She didn't want you to get 'a potbelly.' Her words, not mine."

Ned turned to look at me over his shoulder, surprise

in his eyes. "I could go run around the yard between cram sessions, if it would mean more cookies," he said. "You tell Hannah that."

"I think we're getting off track here," I reminded him.

Ned inhaled another cookie. "I dithagwee," he muttered, spewing crumbs.

I stepped closer, tapping his shoulder. "I came over here to check on the Black Creek Farm test results."

Ned sighed, drawing his fingers over the plastic lock on the bag. "That reminds me," he said sadly. "I should save some of these for Rashid. To say thank you, y'know?"

"Don't bother." I pulled another plastic bag from my other pocket. "I've got you covered. Now, the results?"

Ned put down the bag of cookies and turned to look me in the face. My skin prickled with nerves. I had a feeling, from his very serious brown eyes, that I wasn't going to like whatever he was about to say.

"Rashid said the cooked dishes were all clean," he said. *"But . . ."*

"But?" I prodded, knowing that the important info lay beyond that word.

"But the cold dishes, the salads, were *crawling* with E. coli," Ned finished.

As I nodded slowly, taking this in, Ned reached for the bag and scarfed another cookie.

"Clearly this hasn't affected your appetite," I observed with amusement.

Ned shook his head. "I'm sorry. I'm just starving. I was so busy cramming I sort of forgot to go to the dining hall for breakfast. And then for lunch." He popped another cookie in his mouth.

"Ned, is that all you've eaten today?" I asked.

"Don't be ridiculous," he said. "I also had a bag of Skittles and an energy drink."

I put my hand on Ned's shoulder. "Come on," I said. "Let's go over to the snack bar and get you something *real* to eat."

A few minutes later we sat at a wrought-iron table in the shade just outside the university café. Ned was chomping happily on an enormous chicken burrito, and I sipped an iced tea.

I was trying not to obsess about Rashid's findings. At least, not while Ned was eating. But "not obsessing" about a case I was working on felt like "not breathing" to me. Finally I let out a sigh and leaned forward.

"So the cooked dishes were clean?"

Ned didn't even look surprised. He held up one finger while he swallowed and set his burrito down on a paper plate. "Not clean," he clarified after a few seconds. "Not necessarily. Rashid said that they might have been contaminated too, but the high temperatures of cooking would likely kill off any traces. That's why we're always told to make sure chicken and fish are cooked thoroughly and to avoid eating rare beef."

"So all the vegetables could have been contaminated," I realized. "Does that seem strange? That it would be all of them—not just one or two dishes?"

Ned shrugged, picking up the burrito. "Strange? Sure, maybe a little. But not impossible." He took a bite.

I tapped my finger against my lips, thinking. "But E. coli comes from the digestive system of cows. Sam was right. I researched it last night."

Ned glanced at me briefly before taking another big bite. "Hmmmmmm."

"It couldn't just *show up* on vegetables that are grown nowhere near cows," I went on. "A human being would have to transfer it."

Ned dunked what was left of his burrito in a little puddle of guacamole. "Mm-hmm."

I folded my arms, pondering. I wasn't exactly looking for a case to solve right now. I'd been enjoying a break from sleuthing, taking up tennis, and on George's recommendation (okay, more like insistence), making it halfway through *Lost* on Netflix. I didn't want to give up my free time.

But Sam's defeated expression as I'd walked him to his car last night stuck with me. *This is my dream.* And from what Rashid had found, it seemed very likely that someone was trying to take that dream away from him. *Why?*

"Who hates an organic farm?" I asked.

Ned glanced up from his guacamole, which he was now scooping up with a spoon. "Is that the setup for a joke, Nance?"

I shook my head. "No, I'm serious. If he were still a lawyer, I could see him having enemies. Ooh . . ." I paused, bringing my hand to my mouth. "Maybe that's it? An enemy he made in his law days wants to destroy the thing that matters most to him—*his farm*!"

Ned stuck his finger into the spoon to pick up one last dab of guacamole, then stuck his finger in his mouth. "That's it, Nance," he said, deadpan. "You've solved the case. That must be some kind of record."

I reached out and bopped him on the head. "Stop it," I said. "I'm serious! Who would sabotage an organic farm?"

Ned shrugged. "No one?" he asked. But I recognized an arch tone in his voice, like he was trying to point out something obvious.

"You don't think someone is behind the E. coli?" I asked.

Ned sighed. He reached for his soda and took a long sip. "It's just . . . the guy was a lawyer, and now he's an expert organic farmer?" he asked. "You know about Occam's razor, Nance?"

I nodded. Occam's razor, the principle, actually came up a lot when solving mysteries. "Sure. Occam's razor says that the simplest solution is most likely the correct one."

"So isn't it likely that this guy just screwed up and put something on his plants that he wasn't supposed to?" he asked. "Cow manure. Some kind of unapproved fertilizer. And the plants got contaminated, and that poor woman got sick. Lucky us, we were warned." Ned shrugged again. "Isn't that more likely than some big bad guy sprinkling cow bile on these vegetables to make people sick? To close down a farm? Who would *do* that?"

"I don't know," I said, fishing my phone out of my purse, "but I intend to find out."

I opened the texting application and typed a quick note to Bess and George: YOU GUYS FREE TO GO TO BLACK CREEK FARM TOMORROW?

Ned glanced at the text and pretended to pout. "You're going without me?"

I grinned at him. "You have midterms, remember?"

Ned startled like he'd just been reminded he had a midterm *right then*. His eyes bugged out. "Oh my gosh, you're right! What am I *doing* here, out in the world? Why did you drag me out of my study-hole, temptress?"

I laughed. "You needed to eat. If you faint in the middle of your midterm, it doesn't matter how much you studied."

Ned nodded, sipping his drink. "Your logic is sound."

A *ping!* sounded on my phone, and I looked down to see a text from George: I'M IN! As I typed out a response—GREAT, WILL TXT U DETAILS—Bess responded too: OF COURSE! WHAT TIME?

I fished Sam Heyworth's business card out of my

wallet and dialed the phone number. The phone rang only once before someone picked up.

"Hello?"

It was Abby. And her voice sounded a little tremulous and unsure.

"Hi, Abby? This is Nancy Drew. We met last night?"

"Oh, of course." Abby's voice sounded warmer now.

"Listen, I was wondering if I might set up a time tomorrow to come visit the farm with my friends Bess and George. I'd love to have a look around. Sam and I talked about it a bit last night."

A hollow sigh echoed over the line. "That would be great, Nancy," Abby replied in a serious tone. "In fact, the sooner the better. Something very strange has happened on the farm . . . something awful."

CHAPTER FOUR

~

Lay of the Land

I PULLED INTO THE DRIVEWAY OF BLACK Creek Farm the next morning just after ten o'clock, with Bess in the passenger seat. George, who had to work a shift at the Coffee Cabin that afternoon, was right behind us in her own car. We both parked and climbed out, greeted by a soft breeze and gentle birdsong.

"It's beautiful here," enthused George, taking in the gentle rolling hills shaded by old oak and pine trees. "I can see why Sam would trade some corporate office for this."

"Let's just hope it was the right decision," said Bess.

I followed, taking some time to soak in all the details of the farm. A circular driveway led to a modest white ranch-style house. Behind the house, I could see what looked like fields of corn, lettuce, and some crops I couldn't identify, all stretching over gently rolling hills. The fields were dotted with small storage buildings, a barn, and the occasional piece of farming equipment.

George was right: it was beautiful, and the farm looked idyllic in the midmorning sun. *You'd never guess the crops were crawling with E. coli,* I thought. *Or are they?* It was also possible, I realized, that the vegetables had been contaminated at the dinner itself and there was nothing strange going on at the farm.

"Nancy?"

I came out of my thoughts to find Bess and George watching me, a smile playing on the edges of Bess's lips.

"Do you have it all memorized and filed away?" she teased. Bess had tagged along on enough investigations to be well used to my tendency to observe carefully and make note of little details. "Can we knock on the door now?"

"Knock away," I agreed. We climbed onto the small porch attached to the house, and I raised my fist to knock. Just as my knuckle rapped against the wood, sounds emerged from inside.

"She's not going to eat that!"

Jack. I recognized the voice immediately. I looked awkwardly at my friends, who were both wearing the same *uh-oh* expression that I imagined on my own face.

"Overreacting . . . perfectly safe!"

That sounded like Sam.

"Oh great," Bess murmured, folding her arms. "We've arrived right in the middle of a huge family argument. That's not awkward!"

I lifted a finger to hush her as Jack's voice—louder than Sam's—traveled toward us again.

"Don't you even care about my unborn child? Why risk it?"

I heard the screech of a chair being pushed back quickly, followed by stomping and a female voice making soothing sounds—possibly Julie? I couldn't be sure. I'd barely heard Jack's wife speak at the dinner.

George looked at me quizzically. "Are we waiting for this to be over?" she whispered. "Should we come back another time?"

I shook my head, realizing that made no sense. "No, let's just knock again," I said, frowning. "I don't think they heard us before. And I have a feeling this could go on awhile."

George nodded and lifted her hand to rap sharply on the door: four precise knocks. When we didn't immediately hear footsteps coming toward us, she knocked again, a little louder. There was silence for a moment, and then the scrambling sound of someone rushing to the door. Somebody pulled back the curtain that blocked most of the window in the door, let it fall back, and quickly swung the door open.

"Nancy!"

It was Abby, pink-cheeked and dressed in a neat button-down and jeans.

"I'm so glad you made it! Thank you for stopping by, girls. Please, come on in."

We cautiously followed Abby into the foyer. It was a small, neat, wood-paneled room, holding a table decorated with family photos and ceramic animals. Abby saw me looking at the animals and smiled.

"Those are our farm animals," she said kindly. "I think Sam was a little disappointed that we decided to raise only chickens on the farm. So we got some miniature cows, pigs, and sheep for him to tend."

"Hello, Nancy." At the mention of his name, Sam's booming voice sprang from the doorway that led to the kitchen. "And your friends, Jess and—?"

"Bess," Bess said with a smile, holding out her hand. Sam nodded and shook it.

"And George," George added. "Your farm is beautiful," she said as she and Sam shook hands.

"Thank you very much," he replied. "Yes, it's our own little piece of paradise. Speaking of which, can I offer you some of my famous sweet potato—"

There was a loud groan from the kitchen. *Jack*.

"Dad, just throw them away!" Jack suddenly appeared behind his father, his dark eyes shining. He glanced at us but didn't acknowledge us. "I didn't just mean they're unsafe for *Julie* to eat. I meant they're unsafe for *everyone*."

Sam sighed, his face reddening. He looked uncomfortable.

He wants to throttle Jack, I realized. *But not in front of the three of us.*

"That's a shame," I said quickly, wanting to speak up before Sam or Abby changed the subject. "Sweet potatoes are my *favorite* vegetable. What's wrong with the . . . What kind of dish is it, Sam?"

Sam spoke without taking his eyes off his son. "Pancakes," he replied. "My own recipe. The sweet potatoes are from the farm, of course."

"Which makes them *unsafe*," Jack added, a crimson color spreading over his ears and cheeks. I could make out a vein throbbing in his neck. "Come on, Dad. It isn't rocket science."

"What makes them unsafe?" Sam shot back. I

recognized the same hardness in his dark eyes that I'd seen in Jack's the night of the buffet. *They're both stubborn,* I realized.

"The fact that they're crawling with some kind of contaminant?" Jack replied. "The fact that they made my wife so sick she had to be brought to the ER? Dad, really."

"I washed them thoroughly," Sam insisted. "And I cooked them well."

"It's still a risk!" Jack's voice rose to a yelp.

Abby cleared her throat. All eyes turned to her.

"Why don't we set this subject aside for the moment and invite our *guests* into the kitchen to sit down?" she asked. "Pancakes or no, we have plenty of coffee and fresh blueberry muffins—made with blueberries I *bought*, I should add."

There was silence for a moment, and Bess smiled eagerly. "That sounds great," she said. "Blueberries are *my* favorite vegetable."

Sam chuckled, and Abby and Jack soon joined in. I felt relieved. Bess always seemed to know the right thing to say to lighten the mood.

But Jack glared at Sam as we departed for the kitchen and shook his head. "I'm going out," he muttered. He walked out the front door, and a few seconds later I could hear a car starting up, and then driving down the driveway.

We settled in the kitchen, where Julie, looking much healthier than the last time I had seen her, sat sipping from a mug at the table. There was a plate near the stove piled high with orange pancakes, and a plate sat near the sink, swiped clean, dripping with syrup. I noted a small pile of pancakes in the sink. The pancakes Sam tried to serve Julie, I figured.

Julie gestured to a blueberry muffin sitting on a saucer in front of her. "If it's all the same to you guys, I'll just eat this," she said with a wry smile. "Hello, girls."

"How are you feeling?" Bess asked, moving forward and taking a seat at the table next to Julie.

"*Much* better," Julie replied. "The hospital did a great job of stopping the nausea and keeping me hydrated. But I was still feeling tired until this morning. Now I just feel . . . well, as tired as an eight-months-pregnant woman should feel."

I laughed quietly, along with my friends. George and I took seats at the table, and Abby served us coffee, tea, and warm muffins with butter. The conversation turned to gentler topics, like the weather and what we were studying in school. After a few minutes, Abby turned to Sam. "Why don't you take the girls outside?" she asked. "Show them around. Show them what *happened*."

I glanced at Sam. "Yes, what is it that happened yesterday?" I asked. Abby hadn't given me many details on the phone and had told me it was nothing to worry about, but of course I was worried. Under the circumstances, anything unusual that happened at Black Creek Farm seemed like something to worry about.

Sam shook his head. "It's . . . no big deal," he said. "Just unusual. Yes, girls, if you're finished, perhaps we can head out?"

I glanced at my friends. They made murmurs of

agreement and pushed back from the table. Sam rose and led us to a screen door off the back of the kitchen. We followed him out and onto another low porch, down a ramp, and out toward the fields of crops.

Sam looked up at the sun and let out a satisfied sigh. "What a day, what a day," he murmured. "You don't get weather like *this* on the twenty-sixth floor of an office high-rise, I'll tell you that."

"Why don't you tell us about how you built the farm?" George suggested. "Last night Holly told me that this was all an unused field before you bought it and started building Black Creek Farm. How did you plan it? How did you figure out what to do?"

Sam smiled, surveying the farm with a look of contentment. "Oh," he said. *"Well . . ."*

He went on to tell us a complicated story about agricultural research, irrigation theory, nutritional optimization, and a bunch of other terms I didn't fully understand. But as Sam spoke and lovingly pointed out his fields of greens, corn, peas, eggplants, summer squash, zucchini, and tomatoes, one thing was clear: Sam *really* loved farming and, despite what Jack had said the night of the buffet, had put a *lot* of thought into how his farm would work best. When George asked a throwaway question about why he'd planted greens in a certain field, and not closer to the house, Sam went into a long explanation about hours of direct sunlight, evaporation levels, and soil composition. *He really knows what he's doing,* I realized. I remembered my conversation with Ned the day before: *Isn't it likely that this guy just screwed up and put something on his plants that he wasn't supposed to?*

Sorry, Ned, but I don't think Occam's razor holds up in this case. I watched Sam's eyes light up as he plucked a perfect red tomato from a plant that snaked up a cross-hatch of wire.

That's the thing about solving mysteries. It's not always the simplest solution that turns out to be true.

"Sam, can you tell us more about what happened yesterday?" I asked.

Sam's face fell as he handed the tomato to George.

"Take that home," he encouraged her. "Just . . . be sure to wash it thoroughly."

George nodded, raising her eyebrows at me.

Sam cleared his throat. "The *incident*, if you could call it that . . . it happened over here."

We followed obediently as Sam led us through the tomatoes, up a small hill, past the barn and chicken coop (filled with the trilling, clucking sounds of birds), and toward a large glass greenhouse.

"Oh, you have a greenhouse!" George observed happily. "Does that mean you can grow crops all year long?"

Sam waved his hand to indicate *more or less*. "Almost. Hearty plants like kale and cabbage, beets and parsnips, those do best. But yes, the greenhouse is very helpful. With it, we can produce cucumbers and tomatoes in the spring, and going well into the fall. We can start seeds in a safe, nurturing environment. It was an excellent investment."

He pulled a key from his pocket and fitted it into the lock in the door, twisting and pushing the door open. He walked in, gesturing for us to follow, and I entered first, followed by Bess and then George.

"Oh . . . oh *no!*" George cried. I looked around and realized what my friend was reacting to: the greenhouse had been *trashed.* Dirt, uprooted plants, pots, and trays littered the floor, and it looked like someone had taken the time to carefully rip each plant apart. There were even broken panes in the greenhouse's glass walls.

Bess and I gasped. "When did this happen?" I asked.

Sam shrugged. "Sometime between seven a.m. and three p.m. yesterday," he said. "It was stupid—I always keep this locked, but yesterday morning I forgot. Guess my mind was on other things."

I stepped farther into the greenhouse, trying to take in every detail. As I picked my way through the dirt and shattered pots to the far wall, I caught sight of something that made the hairs on the back of my neck stand up.

"Oh my gosh!" I pointed, and Bess and George ran up behind me to take a look.

Someone had used dirt to scrawl a message on the floor: KILL THE FARM!

George's mouth dropped open. "Sam," she called, "did you see this?"

Sam, who was lingering by the door, moved forward, climbing through the overturned pots to the spot where George was standing. He surveyed the words with a stunned expression. "I'll be . . ." He stopped and shook his head. "No," he said to George. "I didn't see that yesterday."

"It seems like a pretty clear message," I said, stating the obvious.

Sam nodded slowly. "I . . ." He gave a nervous laugh. "It's strange. Of course it makes me angry, seeing this. But it also makes me feel . . ."

"Scared?" asked Bess. I noticed then that she looked a little alarmed. Her blue eyes were wide, her brows raised.

Sam thought a moment. "Not scared, though maybe I should be. No . . . I feel relieved." He chuckled again. "Because this proves it, doesn't it? It proves that

I'm not crazy. Someone out there is trying to sabotage me. Someone out there wants to destroy Black Creek Farm!" He brought his hand down, slapping at the table beside him, strewn with torn-up pepper plants.

"But . . . why?" I asked. I understood what Sam was saying, about the relief. This made it easier for me, in a way: now I just had to find the culprit. But I had a feeling that was going to be the hard part.

Sam sighed, seeming to think. "I . . . don't know," he said finally.

Of course you don't. It's kind of amazing to me, how many people who are being targeted have no idea that anyone's mad at them. And with Sam, I could understand: he seemed like a perfectly nice guy. Who *would* want to destroy a kind man's organic farm?

"You don't have any enemies?" Bess pressed, looking around at the damage.

"I don't." Sam shrugged, as if to say, *What can you do?* "Not that I know of, anyway."

"Maybe someone from your lawyering days?" I suggested. "Someone you defended but couldn't get off? Someone who was on the opposing side of a case you won?"

Sam looked thoughtful, as though he was searching his memory, examining each case one by one. "Every lawyer has those sorts of enemies, if you could call them that," he said. "But I can't think of a single person who might be angry enough to track me down and try to destroy my farm."

Hmmmm. George knelt down and picked up a pepper plant that looked more or less intact, carefully placing it on the table. "What about the farm?" she asked.

"What about it?" Sam asked, confused.

"This might sound strange, but does the *farm* have any enemies?" she asked. "Someone who was inconvenienced, or lost money, when you guys set up the farm here?"

Sam frowned, looking off into space.

"Someone you're competing with?" I prompted. "Maybe a bigger farm nearby?"

"There's a bigger farm down the road, sure, Sunshine

Farm," Sam said. He turned to look me in the eye, and his expression was uncomfortable. "There are farms all over this area. And I did have a brief . . . disagreement, I guess you'd call it, with them."

"What was it?" Bess asked, looking eager.

Sam rolled his eyes. "Oh, it was silly. Just a little thing. They had planted their spinach very close to my berry fields, encroaching onto my land, and the chemicals they treat their crops with were leaching into my strawberries. I couldn't let that go on, since strawberries soak up a lot of chemicals. So I complained to them, and they weren't happy about it, but they eventually had to replant their spinach farther away from my land."

This was intriguing. "Did it cost them money?" I asked. Most of the cases I work on have money at the root of them.

Sam shook his head. "Some, sure. A little. But I really don't think Sunshine Farm is holding a grudge," he said.

Just at that moment, the door to the greenhouse

was pushed open. An older man with leathery tan skin and a grizzled gray beard stood there, wearing a baseball cap and a black hoodie. He looked startled.

"I'm sorry," he said. "I didn't know anyone was in here. . . ."

But Sam was already waving his hand like he was waving away the man's concerns. "Don't worry about it, Bob," he said. He gestured to Bess, George, and me. "These are just friends of mine. They're looking into the vandalism here and what's been happening with the vegetables."

Bob nodded, a little nervously, I thought. "Oh," he said. "Okay." Then, after a few seconds: "It's a terrible thing, what's happening with the vegetables. People getting sick."

"Yes," Sam replied shortly. He turned back to us. "Bob helps us pick the produce when we have a busy week. He lives in town. Rides his motorcycle out here."

Bob nervously fingered the string of his hoodie. He looked at me, like he felt he had to explain himself. "Sam has been very good to me," he said. "I hope you catch whoever's doing the bad stuff."

Huh. I nodded. "Yeeeeeah, I hope I do." I smiled, and he backed away.

"I'll come back later," he called to Sam.

We all watched the doorway after his retreat, and after a few seconds, Sam said quietly, "Bob's had a tough life. He's a Vietnam vet, you know. He's been a little down on his luck, and we can use extra hands on the farm, so I've been paying him to help out on the weekends."

I raised my eyebrows. "You . . . don't think he might . . . ?"

Sam turned to me, his forehead wrinkled with concern. "*Bob?* Oh, gosh. No. He has absolutely no issue with me. I've done nothing but help him."

There was silence for a minute. *So Sam doesn't want me to suspect Bob,* I thought, frowning. *Which makes me even more suspicious.*

"So, why?" Bess asked suddenly, seemingly out of the blue.

Sam looked at her in surprise. "Why have I helped out Bob?" he asked. "I don't know. It seemed like the decent thing to do."

"No." Bess shook her head. "Right before you came in, you were saying you don't think Sunshine Farm holds a grudge. I was just wondering why."

"Oh." Sam laughed, still seeming a little uncomfortable. "Well, in short, because of their daughter," he replied. "Lori Park. You met her at the dinner the other night."

At the dinner. My mind flashed back to the young girl who'd been helping prepare the food. "The girl around our age who was working in the kitchen?" I asked.

"She's the one," he said. "Lori's parents are from Korea, and there was a bit of a language barrier, so when we were having our little disagreement, Lori was called in to act as a translator." He smiled. "It turns out she has a real interest in environmental, sustainable farming. She convinced her parents that what I'm doing at Black Creek Farm is worthwhile. Even tried to convince them to try organic farming, but they didn't want to mess with what works, you know."

"She wanted them to go organic?" George asked.

Sam nodded. "She's a very clever girl, too. Came up with all these monetary reasons, did up this

PowerPoint presentation. But they still said no."

"That's a shame," I said.

Sam shrugged. "Well, I can understand it. Anyway, it all worked out. She comes over a few times a week to help us out and learn more about organic farming. She's headed to the University of California next year to study agriculture."

"Wow," Bess said, sounding impressed. But I was only half listening. While Sam had been talking, I'd noticed something peeking out from underneath a pile of shattered clay pots and soil. It was bright blue, shiny . . .

I scurried over and lifted the object between two careful fingers. It was a pair of sunglasses with bright-blue frames. I held them up so Sam could see them.

"Do you recognize these?" I asked. "Because it's fair to say, whoever owns these was in the greenhouse recently."

"Oh." Sam looked at the glasses, and his face fell. He seemed to deflate like a beach ball with the stopper pulled out.

"Those are Lori's sunglasses."

CHAPTER FIVE

Revelations

"I HATE TO GO, GUYS." GEORGE BIT HER lip as she, Bess, and I all stood in the Heyworths' driveway again. George was leaving, heading back to River Heights so she could make her shift as barista and waitress at the Coffee Cabin.

"Maybe I should go with you." Bess, who'd been twisting a lock of blond hair around her index finger, suddenly spoke up. "I kind of wanted to get a manicure today."

"Are you *kidding* me?" I turned to my friend, surprised and annoyed. "I'm about to go question Lori

Park about why her sunglasses were in Sam's recently vandalized greenhouse. You don't want to see what happens?"

Bess sighed. "I just . . ." She shook her head. "I'm not as into this farming stuff as you guys. I want Sam to find out who's sabotaging his farm, but . . ."

George rolled her eyes. "Stay here and help Nancy, please. I feel bad enough that I can't."

"All *right.*" Bess sighed again, but her frustrated tone told me that she was feeling a little guilty too. "Let's go, then." She started heading toward the road. Sunshine Farm, Sam had told us, was just half a mile away, an easy walk.

"Wait," George said, lifting a basket of vegetables from her passenger seat. "Remind me what you want me to ask Ned to tell Rashid? We're testing these for E. coli?"

"That's right," I said. Since she was heading back to River Heights, George had offered to bring some more vegetables to Rashid for testing. "These are straight from the farm, just picked. Ask him if Rashid can test them for E. coli and tell us what he finds out. If these veggies are contaminated already, then we'll know whoever's sabotaging the crops is doing it here, at the farm."

George nodded. "Got it," she said, replacing the basket on her passenger seat and closing the door. She walked around to the driver's side. "I'll ask Ned to call or text as soon as he knows. Okay?"

"Okay," I agreed.

"And you call *me*," George added, pointing at me, "as soon as you figure out who's harassing Sam. Deal?"

"Deal!" I agreed, giving George a thumbs-up. She climbed into her car and started up the engine as I followed Bess down the driveway to the road. As we walked, George passed us in her little coupe, tooting the horn. We both waved.

It was a pleasant enough walk down the road, surrounded by fields of corn. On the left side, a big hand-painted sign welcomed us to SUNSHINE FARM— WHERE WE HARNESS THE SUN FOR YOU! The words were surrounded by glossy-looking paintings of tomatoes, eggplants, zucchini, and peaches.

A driveway led to a bustling farm stand, brimming with flowers and produce. It took a while for me to get the attention of a cashier, but when I asked, she suggested that we look for Lori in the cherry orchard.

"Take a right on the road by the swing set," she said brusquely. "It's about a quarter mile down. There'll be lots of people picking there today."

We followed her instructions. Sunshine Farm made Black Creek Farm look downright sleepy by comparison. Farmhands worked in an outbuilding sorting tomatoes, and as we walked along the path to the orchard, a tractor passed us, hauling a trailer filled with buckets of cherries.

Bess let out a little moan. "Seeing all those delicious fruits and veggies at the farm stand reminded me how hungry I am," she said.

"We'll have to grab a snack on our way out," I suggested.

"Maybe," Bess said, turning her attention to the cherry orchard that we were approaching. Rows of trees stretched back toward the horizon, many with ladders leaning against them and farmworkers standing on rungs near the tops, picking cherries and placing them in buckets that hung from the branches. The cherries were bright scarlet, shiny in the midday sun. They contrasted nicely against the emerald-green leaves of the tree. I wasn't even that hungry, but the sight of them made my mouth water. "Or maybe," said Bess, "I'll just grab a sample."

She ran up to the closest tree and leaned up as far as she could, plucking a trio of cherries from a low branch. "Mmmmm," Bess murmured, popping one into her mouth. But almost immediately, her mouth puckered.

"Ugh!" she cried, spitting the chewed-up cherry into her hand.

"Yup," a female voice suddenly spoke up from behind me. I turned to find the same young girl we'd seen working in the kitchen at the Black Creek buffet. She looked amused. "Those are sour cherries."

Bess spat out the juice onto the grass. "Why would anyone grow *sour* cherries?" she asked.

The girl laughed. "They're not so sour when you bake them into a pie or cook them into jam with lots of sugar," she said. "They're just not so tasty right off the tree. Anyway, can I help you? I'm Lori."

I smiled. "Hi, I'm Nancy, and my hungry friend's name is Bess. You might remember seeing us at the Black Creek Farm dinner the other night."

Bess's cheeks blushed nearly the color of the cherries. "Hi," she said. "I don't usually steal cherries."

Lori nodded. "I believe you," she said, very seriously. Then we all laughed.

"I'm here because I wanted to ask you about what's been going on at Black Creek Farm," I said.

Lori's expression turned solemn. "You mean what happened at the buffet the other night, with Julie getting sick?" she asked. "That was terrible."

I exchanged a glance with Bess. *She's acting like she doesn't know about the vandalism.* But was it an act?

I held up the pair of blue sunglasses I'd found in the greenhouse. "Um, do you recognize these?"

Lori's eyes flashed with recognition. "Sure. Those

are mine. I must have left them at the farm yesterday morning."

I handed them to her. "Where were you working yesterday?"

Lori took the sunglasses and put them on top of her head. "Kind of all over. I was picking sweet potatoes, and then I was in the greenhouse for a while."

"Did you notice anything unusual at the greenhouse?" I asked. The vandalism we'd seen that day was certainly *unusual*. But also, if she was behind it, I expected to see a flash of discomfort cross Lori's face—the realization that her crime had been discovered.

She just looked at me blankly, though. "Oh, the door was unlocked," she said after a few seconds. "That's a little weird, because Sam usually locks it."

"Did you lock it when you finished?" I asked.

Lori shook her head. "I was worried maybe he'd left it unlocked for a reason," she explained. "Like he or Bob had forgotten their keys. So when I was finished working in there, I left the door unlocked."

Hmmmm. I glanced at Bess, who raised her eyebrows at me.

"And it seemed . . . totally normal when you left?" I asked.

Lori looked like she was beginning to wonder where these questions were coming from. "It looked totally normal," she affirmed. "Um, why are you asking?"

Bess cleared her throat. "Nancy's trying to get to the bottom of what happened at the buffet," she explained breezily. "She's, like, a teenage sleuth." She made a big show of looking over at me and then back at Lori and shrugging, like *What can you do?* "Keeps her off the streets," she added.

Lori smiled. "Um, is that a real thing? Teenage sleuth?"

While I turned red, Bess grinned and leaned close to Lori. "I know, it sounds like a bad TV series or something, right?" she asked. "Anyway, do you work for the Heyworths a lot? Sam says you're into organic farming."

Lori nodded. "Yeah, I kind of wish my parents would give it a shot here, but they're afraid they'd lose money."

"What's so much better about organic?" Bess asked. Her tone was totally casual, but I could see the focus in her eyes. She was information-gathering.

"It's better for everyone, basically," Lori said, her dark eyes serious. "It's less harmful to the environment, to wild animals. It's more sustainable. And there's some evidence that the produce is actually more nutritious."

"I thought those studies were inconclusive," I piped up, channeling Ned.

Lori rolled her eyes. "They're conclusive enough for me," she said. "So yeah, since my parents wouldn't budge, I spend some time at Sam's farm volunteering and learning how organic farming works."

"Do you want to be a farmer?" Bess asked.

"Eventually," she said, "definitely. I have a year of high school left, and then I want to go to college to study agriculture. My plan is, after that, I'll work at other organic farms until I can raise enough money to start my own."

Bess smiled encouragingly. "You don't think your parents would let you run part of theirs?"

Lori shrugged, then looked away. "Maybe," she admitted. "If I come back with a college degree and *still* say we should go organic, maybe they'd take me more seriously." She paused, looking from Bess to me. "Hey, have you guys been at Black Creek today?" she asked.

Bess and I said that we had.

"How's Julie doing?" Lori asked, her expression serious again. "She was still kind of weak yesterday."

"She's better," I explained. "It looks like she had E. coli poisoning."

"E. coli?" Lori asked, her voice as incredulous as if I'd just said that Julie had bubonic plague. "Julie got *E. coli* from Sam's produce?"

"Yep," I said, watching Lori's eyes carefully. She looked completely stunned.

"How?" she asked.

"We don't know," I said honestly. "Do you?"

She shook her head, then brought her hand to her mouth. "It just . . . it doesn't make sense."

Bess glanced at me, then back at Lori. "Is there any chance," she said, "that the food was contaminated at the community center?"

Lori's eyes looked unfocused as she thought. "I guess it's possible," she said finally, "but not on my watch. Holly and I were really careful. I worked in a restaurant last summer; I know about safe food preparation." She paused. "Really, this just doesn't make sense."

"Do you think that maybe the produce was contaminated on the farm?" I suggested.

Lori frowned, looking back at me. "I guess," she said, "but *how*? Sam runs a clean farm. It would be really weird for *any* bacteria to show up on his produce, much less E. coli. You know E. coli comes from animals, right? And Sam only keeps a few chickens."

I nodded, looking down at the ground, and when I did so I noticed a smartphone peeking out of the top of Lori's jeans pocket. It shouldn't have surprised me;

every kid our age carried his or her smartphone every-where, all the time. Even working on a farm. But it *did* give me an idea.

"Oh, gosh," I said, trying to look like I'd just remembered something. "I totally forgot that I need to call my dad and tell him I won't be able to meet him for lunch in half an hour. But I left my phone back at Sam's. Does anyone have one I can borrow?"

Bess looked at me, amused. I knew her phone was in her purse, but she'd seen me pull the "borrow your phone" maneuver enough times to know that she should *not* offer it to me. Lori looked from me to Bess, then reached into her pocket with an easy shrug.

"Sure, here's mine," she said, handing her smart-phone over. *Success!* "Let me just type in the pass code . . . there."

"Thanks," I said sincerely. "I'm just going to, um, take this over there"—I gestured to a picnic table behind a small copse of trees—"so you don't hear him lecture me about changing plans at the last minute. *Soooo* embarrassing!"

Lori and Bess nodded understandingly as I took the phone and darted over to the tables, out of sight. I heard Bess asking Lori a question about her school's football team as I made my escape. *That's it, Bess, cover for me,* I thought as I sat down and looked at the phone. As much as Bess hadn't wanted to come along on this interview mission, she was doing an amazing job of cozying up to Lori and getting information.

I went to the phone's history first: recent calls and voice mails. There was one voice mail from yesterday, but when I listened to it, it was just a classmate asking Lori for the algebra homework assignment. None of the placed calls looked unusual—all local, within our area code. No familiar names in her contact list aside from Sam Heyworth.

So I went to texts. There were several from the day before, setting up a meeting with her friend Haley at the library to study after she finished at Black Creek Farm. A couple of texts to her mother, updating her on where Lori was. Nothing seemed unusual, and nothing seemed to contradict Lori's story that she'd left the greenhouse looking fine—but unlocked. A quick search through her personal e-mails turned up a crush on a classmate named Jason, but no useful information having to do with Black Creek.

So far there was no proof that anyone at Sunshine Farm had sabotaged Black Creek Farm.

I hid any signs of my snooping and walked back to Lori and Bess, holding out the phone.

". . . I don't know," Lori was saying with a shy smile, "*maybe* he likes me? But it's so hard to tell. I've known him since I was, like, in diapers."

"If only boys would tell us what they were thinking, huh?" Bess replied sympathetically. "But maybe that would make it too easy."

"Easy is good for me. I like easy," Lori said. She looked up as I approached. "Did you get your dad?"

I nodded. "Yeah, he was actually fine with it. Thank goodness!"

Lori took the phone from my hand with a smile and tucked it back into her pocket. I glanced at Bess and raised an eyebrow, trying to send the message: *Did you find out anything suspicious?*

Bess gave a very tiny shake of her head and widened her eyes. *No, she seems totally normal. I don't know what to do.*

I cleared my throat. "Listen, Lori," I said, "something actually happened at Black Creek Farm yesterday that has Sam kind of rattled."

"Really?" Lori looked surprised. "More than just Julie being sick?"

"Yeah." I let out a breath. "The thing is, someone vandalized the greenhouse yesterday. Probably sometime after you left. Which was?"

Lori blinked at me, surprised. "Ah . . . about noon, maybe? Wait, what do you mean, *vandalized*?"

"Someone went in there and knocked over all the plants," Bess explained. "Really tore them up, left a huge mess of broken pots and dirt all over the floor. And he or she left a *message*," she added, raising her eyebrows.

"Message?" Lori looked totally confused. "What kind of message? 'I hate plants'?"

"No," I told her. "Someone wrote out 'Kill the farm!' with dirt."

Lori lifted her lip in a sneer. *"Kill the farm?"* she asked. "Seriously?"

I nodded. "Seriously."

Lori let a breath out through her mouth. "I don't even know what to say," she said. Then her eyes darkened. She frowned, looking up at us. "Wait—do you guys think *I* did it?" she asked. "Is that why you came over here?"

I sighed. "Honestly? Yes, it's why we came over here. But I don't really think you did it anymore, after talking to you."

Lori pinched her mouth to the side, thinking that over. "Good," she said after a few seconds, "because I would *never* do something like that to Sam. Gosh, especially now . . ."

Especially now? I guessed she must mean so soon after the disaster of the buffet dinner. I remembered what Sam had said at the time, that Black Creek Farm needed more CSA members and higher sales. This must be a super-stressful time for the whole Heyworth family.

"Do you know who would?" I asked. It had been a minute or so since Lori last spoke, and she looked at me blankly, clearly not sure what I meant.

"Who would what?"

"Who would do something like that to Sam," I clarified. "You know, wrecking his greenhouse. Who would hate an organic farm enough to write 'Kill the farm!' in dirt on the floor?"

Lori shook her head. She was looking off into the distance, thinking hard. She wrinkled her nose slightly, like she could just sniff out who might be that crazy, and didn't like it at all. Then her gaze returned to me, and her expression was blank again.

"I'm really not sure," she said.

She's hiding something. "But if you had to guess?" I prompted.

Lori glanced at her shoes and sighed deeply. Then she looked up at me, meeting my eyes with her serious brown ones. "I don't really know anyone who I think would do this," she said, "*but . . .*"

"But?"

Lori crossed her arms uncomfortably. "But there's been some weird tension with Jack, ever since he arrived," she said finally.

I glanced at Bess.

"Yeah, we've noticed," Bess said in a confidential tone. "He seemed kind of upset this morning. Sam had tried to serve some vegetables from the farm at breakfast, I guess."

Lori nodded. "Yeah, that's not surprising. I saw him yesterday, and he was *really* upset about what happened to Julie. He kept talking about the farm like it was a joke, and the produce was poison or something."

"Well, to Julie it was," I pointed out. Not that I condoned Jack's mean behavior—but I could understand his worry about his wife.

"It's not just that," Lori said, shaking her head. "He's always talking about what a bad investment the farm was. He seems really mad that it's losing money."

Hmmmm. "Why would he care?" I asked. "It's Sam's money to lose, right?"

Lori looked really uncomfortable. She glanced down at her hands and brought a finger to her mouth to nibble on the nail. "Well," she said, "with Sam being sick, you know . . ."

What?

"Wait," I said, holding up my hand. "What do you mean, Sam being sick?"

Lori dropped her hand and looked at me, surprised. "Sam has cancer," she said matter-of-factly. "In his throat, I think. He starts chemo in July. Which has made him even more determined to make the farm work *now*, this year, in case . . ."

Her voice faded out.

Everyone was quiet for a minute as I tried to absorb this information. Sam . . . was *sick*? It made a horrible sort of sense, but it still stunned me.

And Jack's worried about his inheritance, I realized with a shock. *That's what Lori thinks.*

My stomach flipped over. Suddenly the argument

in the kitchen this morning seemed much nastier than I'd first assumed.

"Wow," Bess whispered finally, and I looked at her and nodded.

"Wow," I echoed. "Well, one thing's for sure. This case is even more important now. Whoever's sabotaging Black Creek Farm had better watch out . . . because I don't care what it takes. I'm going to find them!"

CHAPTER SIX

~

One Man's Dream

"DO YOU STILL WANT TO GO HOME?" I ASKED
Bess as we walked back up the road toward Black Creek
Farm. "I'm going to be here for a while, I think. Maybe
it was silly of me to try to get you to come with me to
talk to Lori. I could drive you home and come back. . . ."

Bess put her hand on my arm, stopping me. "Don't
be silly, Nancy," she said. "Of course I'm going to stay.
I'm *invested* now."

She smiled at me, and I smiled back. "I really want
to solve this," I said softly, knowing that I didn't really
need to say it.

"We will," Bess said, looking like she didn't doubt it for a minute. "Of course we will, Nancy. When's the last time Nancy Drew didn't solve her case?"

I nodded but let out a little sigh. It was true, I had a good track record. But it wasn't like I never screwed up. *And I can't afford to screw up this one,* I thought.

The Heyworths' house was quiet when we got back. I knocked gently on the front door, and Abby answered, holding her finger in front of her mouth in the universal *be quiet* gesture. "Sam's napping," she said quietly. "Or as he puts it, 'lying down.' He'd never admit that he needs a nap in the afternoon these days."

I glanced at Bess. *Because he's sick,* I wanted to say. But now seemed like the wrong time to bring it up. Bess nodded almost imperceptibly.

"Oh, you girls must be starving!" Abby said suddenly. "I just realized the time. Won't you come into the kitchen with me? I can make you sandwiches." She turned and headed toward the kitchen, then paused and said over her shoulder, "All store-bought ingredients, I promise."

Bess and I chuckled awkwardly.

"I actually wish we could eat some of the produce from the farm," I said as we filed into the kitchen and took seats at the old farmhouse table. "It all looks delicious."

"It is," a new voice said, and we turned to see Julie entering from the same door we'd just come in, holding a paperback. "Sorry to startle you! I was just reading on the porch and heard voices. I thought I'd come in and see if I might get a cup of tea."

Abby turned to her with a warm smile. "Julie, you know you don't have to ask," she said. "If I can't get my daughter-in-law and the future mother of my grand-child a cup of tea, then I'm not good for much, am I?"

Julie smiled and walked over, giving Abby a quick hug. "Thanks, Mom," she said.

Julie came over to the table and settled down in a chair at the end. "How are you girls?" she asked, brushing her long hair behind her ear and placing her book down on the table. "Did Sam take you to see the greenhouse?"

"He did," I said with a nod. "It's—terrible."

Julie snorted. "I can't imagine what would inspire someone to do that," she said. "An *organic farm*? This whole thing is just so weird."

"Very weird," Bess said with a nod. "And . . ."

She came to a sudden, awkward stop. I met her eye and could tell that she'd been about to say something along the lines of, *And with Sam sick . . .*

I cleared my throat, looking from Julie to Abby. "Um, listen . . . I don't know whether we're supposed to know this or not. . . ."

I trailed off, and Abby turned around from the counter where she'd been making cold-cut sandwiches. Julie looked at me curiously.

I took a deep breath. ". . . but Lori mentioned that Sam has cancer," I finished.

Abby's eyes dimmed. Julie looked down at her hands.

"It's true," Abby said quietly. "I'm sorry—we weren't trying to keep it from you. Sam doesn't like to tell anyone he doesn't have to." She paused, then snorted. "He doesn't want anyone to treat him with pity, he says.

He wants to be treated like he's totally capable until he . . . isn't, anymore."

Bess and I exchanged sad glances. "We're very sorry to hear it," said Bess.

"It was a big blow to the family," Julie said, nervously twirling her hair around her finger. "Coming right after Sam opened his dream farm, and with the first grandchild on the way . . ."

"It's *dreadful* timing," Abby said with a rueful laugh, leaning over to place plates holding turkey-and-swiss sandwiches in front of me and Bess. "But from what I gather, cancer is known for its terrible timing."

I nodded slowly. "I—will he—" *Will he be okay?* was what I wanted to ask. But I realized halfway through the question that it was insensitive. What if the answer was no?

Abby looked at me with understanding. "He starts chemo in July," she said gently. "It has a good chance of shrinking or eradicating the cancer. But of course, no one can say for sure."

I picked up my sandwich and took a tiny nibble. I

wasn't feeling terribly hungry, actually. I glanced at Bess and saw that she was taking the same small, polite bites that I was. *Funny how bad news can destroy your appetite.*

Abby sat down at the table, putting on an enthusiastic expression. "Did you find out anything today, girls?" she asked hopefully. "Do you have any theories about the vegetables?"

I put down my sandwich, chewing and swallowing carefully as I parsed my words. "We've made some good progress," I said. "George took some vegetables from the farm to be tested for E. coli. We'll know more when we hear from her."

Abby nodded. The teakettle whistled, and she started to get up, but Julie jumped up and headed to the stove before her mother-in-law could push back her seat. "Stay where you are," Julie said. "I can get my own tea."

Abby let out a sigh. She looked tired suddenly and placed her elbows on the table, leaning forward to rest her head in her hands. "We have to catch this person," she said. "This farm is Sam's dream. I don't want anyone to keep him from enjoying it for . . . for whatever time he has left," she said, her voice breaking on the last word.

I watched her sympathetically. "Sam told me the farm was losing money?" I said, remembering what Lori had mentioned about the strange tension with Jack.

Abby pulled her hands away and looked me in the eye. "We've been losing money since the farm opened," she said. "But you know what? I don't care about money. I'd rather have a farm that loses money but makes Sam happy than have him working a job that makes us lots of money, but he hates."

How to say this? "It . . . sounds like Jack doesn't feel the same way," I said carefully.

Julie was bringing her tea back to the table, and she and Abby met eyes and exchanged a knowing look as she pulled back her chair and sat down.

"I wish I could say that wasn't true," Abby said. "But . . ."

Julie carefully sipped her tea. "They're so much alike," she said simply, "Jack and Sam."

"They always have been," Abby agreed, her eyes

growing warm with the memory. "Sometimes, I think that's why they butt heads."

Julie turned back to me and Bess. "They're both so *stubborn*," she said, rolling her eyes. "Men!"

Abby laughed.

"So *unreasonable*," Julie added with a smile, sipping her tea again. She leaned back in her chair and added, "And I think Jack was a little hurt when Sam decided to give up practicing law."

"Why?" Bess asked curiously.

"Because Jack is a lawyer too. He followed in his father's footsteps," Abby explained.

"And I think," Julie went on, "that when Sam announced that he didn't want to be a lawyer anymore— that he no longer saw value in that—Jack viewed it as a rebuke."

Abby nodded slowly. "On some level," she said, "I think Jack thinks his father has chosen this farm over him."

Julie looked uncomfortable. "In some ways that's true," she said quietly, gazing down at her tea.

Abby glanced over at her. "What do you mean?"

Julie shrugged, still not meeting her gaze. "Oh, you know," she said lightly. "*I* don't feel this way. But you could argue that Sam's spending money on the farm that Jack might have inherited someday. Anyway, I'm sure Jack will come around."

Abby stared at Julie in surprise, and Bess met my eye with an *Oh no, she didn't* sort of expression. Everything got really quiet. But Julie just kept sipping her tea, as if nothing incredibly awkward had just been said.

Thank goodness my phone beeped right at that moment, cutting the silence. I reached into my pants pocket and pulled it out, excited to see a text from George.

"Oh! This is from my friend who had the vegetables tested," I said eagerly. "She says . . ."

I read the text out loud.

"'Rashid says the veggies were "crawling with" E. coli. So the bad guy is working on the farm? Ugh, wish I weren't working!'"

I lowered my phone and looked up at the faces

around me. Bess looked thoughtful; Julie and Abby looked confused.

"She means the vegetables we picked here on the farm already had E. coli on them," I explained. "Which would seem to imply . . ."

". . . whoever's contaminating the vegetables is doing it here," Bess finished for me.

I nodded. "Right."

Abby and Julie still looked mystified. "So they're doing it *on purpose*," Abby said, not sounding entirely sure.

"It looks that way," I said, taking a deep breath. "Do you know *anyone*—anyone at all—who might wish the farm ill? Who's had access to the plants?"

Abby seemed to think for a while. "No," she said finally.

"Do you have any farmhands?" Bess asked. "Anyone besides Lori and Bob who regularly work on the farm?"

Abby shook her head. "We can't afford them on what we're making," she said. "Lori comes on weekends, and Bob helps out a few times a week, but other than them it's just me and Sam tending the crops. And Jack, since he's been staying here," she added. She straightened up. "Sometimes we get volunteers from the CSA," she said, "but we haven't had anyone out here in weeks."

Everyone was quiet for a minute.

"How would you even *do* it?" Julie asked.

Bess nodded. "Contaminating a whole farm full of produce—in broad daylight? It seems impossible."

I stood up, an idea taking root. "It probably is," I said, walking toward the window and looking out over the rows of crops. *Whoever's doing this is doing it at night,* I realized, and suddenly our next step became clear. I turned to Bess with a grin.

Alarm brightened her eyes. "I know that grin," Bess said. "I hate that grin. That's the 'Nancy has an idea Bess is going to hate' grin."

I shrugged, glancing at the crops again and back.

"So what is it?" Bess went on.

I smiled, gesturing toward the planted fields. "Feel like camping out tonight, Bess?"

~

CHAPTER SEVEN

Trouble in the Barn

"I HATE THIS," BESS GRUMPED AS SHE LAID out one of the sleeping bags Sam and Abby had loaned us in the tent they'd also loaned us.

"Come on, Bess," I chided, bumping her shoulder playfully (which was super easy to do, since the tent was only about five feet across). "We got to have a hot dog cookout for dinner!"

She rolled her eyes. "Yeah, that really made my day, Nancy. Because I am nine years old."

"Anyway," I said, fluffing my pillow, "I thought you were invested in the case now?"

Bess groaned. "Couldn't I be *invested* while we watched the footage from a video camera or something?"

I shook my head. "There's no way a video camera could cover the same amount of space as two sets of human eyes and ears," I explained. "Besides, I want to catch whoever is doing this quickly! The sooner we get this figured out, the sooner everything can go back to normal at Black Creek Farm."

"And with Sam," Bess added quietly, her face drooping.

"And Sam," I confirmed. The kindly farmer had seemed sort of embarrassed when he'd learned that Bess and I knew he had cancer. He apologized for not telling us but repeated what Abby had said—he didn't want anyone to treat him any differently. And he thought it was irrelevant to the case.

But is it? I bit my lip now, remembering how upset Jack had seemed that morning, and even earlier, the night of the buffet. It had been perfectly clear that Jack didn't support his father's decision to become a farmer.

Could he really care more about his inheritance than his father's happiness? I wondered. *Does he think if he ruins Black Creek's reputation, Sam will close the farm and stop losing money by chasing his dream?*

Bess yawned loudly, cutting off my gloomy train of thought. I turned and found her stretched out on her sleeping bag.

"How are we doing this?" she asked, propping herself up on her elbow.

"We take shifts," I explained. We'd discussed this over hot dogs, but I was getting the sense that Bess was pretty worn out. I should have been too, but I guessed adrenaline was keeping me going. *The thrill of the chase.* "Two hours each. I can take the first shift," I offered. "You go to sleep. It's ten now—I'll wake you up at midnight. Okay?"

"Okay," Bess agreed. But her voice was muffled as she was already climbing into her sleeping bag. Abby had loaned us T-shirts and sweatpants to sleep in. It was slightly cool in the tent; perfect sleeping weather.

"I'll sit outside," I said, climbing out the tent's

zippered door. We'd set up the tent on a small hill that overlooked the fields of crops—as close to having a view of the whole farm as I could find.

I settled myself on a rock next to a tree and turned to position an old camping lantern the Heyworths had lent me. I kept the lantern off so our campsite wouldn't attract any attention; the moon was nearly full, casting plenty of light to see into the fields. It was totally quiet except for the occasional hoot of an owl or chirping of crickets. I glanced over at the house; all the lights were out except one, on the top floor. I watched a figure pass in front of the window: Jack. I shuddered and wasn't sure why. Jack had finally returned to the farm as we were finishing up our weenie roast on the back porch. He claimed he'd been working in a coffee shop all day—trying to collect his head. No one questioned him, and he asked where Julie was and then disappeared upstairs. Sam had looked after him, pensive, and Abby had put her hand on his arm and told him to "give Jack time."

Then the conversation had shifted.

The figure disappeared from the window, and soon after, the light went out. Everyone would be going to sleep now—except me.

I cast my eyes out over the fields again. *Where are you, little crops poisoner?* I thought. *Greenhouse destroyer? Dream trampler?*

I rested my back against the tree and got ready for a long night.

It was almost midnight. I stared into my phone, watching each minute pass, dying to wake up Bess so I could get some shut-eye. It had been a long day, and adrenaline could only get me so far.

That was when I heard what sounded like a car coming up the road. My heart squeezed. There were only two farms and one or two other houses on this road—what were the chances someone could be coming home this late? I blinked my eyes and shook my head, trying to wake up. *Could this be my crops saboteur?*

I got to my feet. The car noise died down right in front of the farm. I heard the shuddery sound of an engine turning off, and then a car door opening and slamming.

Gulp. I ran my fingers over the phone in my hand. I'd typed in the farm's house number as a "favorite." The plan was, if I saw anything unusual, I would call and wake them up.

Should I call now?

It was unusual to have someone pull up to the house in the middle of the night, wasn't it?

I swiped my finger across the bottom of the screen to wake up the phone, but before I could enter my pass code, I heard them.

Footsteps.

They were headed from the house . . . *this way.*

I turned and squinted toward the path that led from the driveway, behind the house, to the foot of the hill where we were camped. There it was: a dark figure. It looked small, like a teenager or petite woman, and it wore a gray sweatshirt and a baseball cap. It was carrying something large and heavy-looking in its arms.

Whoever it was, he or she was close enough that they would be upon me before I could get Sam or Abby out here. My fingers clutched uselessly at my phone. *Should I call the police?* I thought of the unlit lantern sitting nearby and considered grabbing it.

But it was too late. I heard a twig snap just feet away and realized the person was already climbing the hill. *It's like they know we're here!* I felt my heart start to pound in my chest.

"Bess!" I tried to shout, but my voice came out as a husky whisper. *This is like a nightmare!* With my last remaining wits, I scrambled back to the tent and reached inside for the item Sam had insisted on loaning us before he went to bed . . .

. . . a baseball bat.

The thing was aluminum and super heavy. Sam said it had belonged to Jack. I raised it over my head and forced air into my lungs, so I could shout . . .

"STAY BACK! I HAVE A WEAPON!"

The figure stopped short. He or she was just a few yards away now, down the hill. I was peering down at the top of a dark baseball cap. *Jack?*

"Nancy?"

The figure spoke in a female voice. It took me a few seconds to realize that this was a *familiar* female voice. She reached up and pulled off the baseball cap, revealing a mop of short-cropped black hair.

"George!" I dropped the baseball cap and lunged toward her, folding her into a hug. (I'm not normally the huggy type, but it's funny what thinking you're in mortal peril will do to you.) "Oh my gosh, you scared me! What are you *doing* here?"

George pulled back and retrieved her phone from her sweatshirt pocket. "I'm sorry, Nancy! I've just been getting all these texts from you and Bess about how you were camping out here tonight. I was feeling a little left out. So when I finished my shift at the Coffee Cabin, I ran home, packed a bag, and drove over. It never occurred to me that you might think I was the bad guy. I'm really sorry."

I let out a sigh of relief. "It's fine, George. Actually . . . I'm really glad you're here."

George smiled. She shifted her arms, and I could see now that the heavy-looking thing she was carrying was just her duffel bag.

I took a step back toward the tent. "Come on in. It's time for me to wake up Bess for her shift."

George raised her eyebrows. "Want me to take the next shift instead?"

"Aren't you tired?"

George shook her head. "It's the benefit of working at a place called the Coffee Cabin, Nance," she said with a smile. "I made myself a double espresso right before I left."

Who knows how many hours later, I startled awake to a sharp poke in the shoulder.

"Your turn," Bess said gruffly. I'd barely woken up enough to hear George come into the tent and wake Bess at two a.m. Before I could respond, she'd already dived around me into her sleeping bag and had the blanket pulled up over her head.

I shimmied out, reached beneath my pillow for

my phone, and checked the time. Four a.m. I glanced over at the other sleeping bag and saw George snoring away.

"Did you see anything?" I asked Bess. My eyes were dying to close again so I could slip back into a dream. I shook my head, trying to clear the cobwebs.

"Nothing," Bess mumbled. "Now I'm enjoying the sight of the insides of my eyelids."

"Gotcha." I let out a final sigh and then drew myself to my feet and scooted out of the tent.

The world outside was dead quiet now. Even the crickets and owls had called it a night, it seemed. I breathed in the cold, clear air and looked around. The moon hung just above the horizon, ready to cede the sky to the sun. A barely perceptible glow of grayish-blue light hovered over the horizon opposite. Sunrise couldn't be far off.

The crops were quiet, seemingly undisturbed. I yawned, wondering whether this was a bad idea. *Maybe whoever's contaminating the crops knows I'm looking into it, so they're keeping quiet.* I frowned. *Maybe whoever's behind it is sleeping right there in that house,* I thought, looking over at the farmhouse.

The house was totally dark. I moved around to make myself comfortable, leaning back against the tree and pulling my sweatshirt around me like a blanket.

Only a few more hours to go . . .

I woke suddenly to dark-blue sky streaked with orange. I jumped up: *What? Where am . . .* But then I looked around and saw the fields of crops spreading out below, the tent with my two sleeping friends inside behind me. *I must have dozed off.* I wiggled around, trying to wake up. *I hope I didn't miss anything. What if—*

CRASH!

I jumped and turned toward the source of the noise. It was coming from behind the storage barn. I got to my feet, hearing the panicked clucking of chickens. *The chicken coop. Someone's spooking the chickens.*

The sun hadn't yet crested the horizon, but the moon was gone. Streaks of orange and pink lit up the sky, but the world still looked dim and ink-stained. I squinted toward the path that led to the storage barn but couldn't make out anything unusual. *Should I call Sam? What if it is Sam?* I pulled out my phone and checked it: 4:53. *Maybe they always feed the chickens at this hour.* Sam and Abby had made jokes the day before about how early the day started on a farm. *Why didn't I ask?*

A shriek sounded from behind the coop, followed by more panicked clucking. I quickly grabbed the lantern, turned it on, and started to run down the hill, then paused. *Should I wake up Bess and George?*

Whatever was going on in the chicken coop, it clearly *wasn't* someone poisoning the crops. *I'll go check it out quickly. It could just be an animal—or a family member feeding them.* The chickens sounded upset, but my dealings with chickens so far had convinced me they weren't the brightest of animals. I wasn't ready to sound the alarm over a few angry chickens.

I shoved my phone into my pocket and scurried down the hill, trying not to make a sound. I darted into the storage barn, which was completely dark except for the glow from my lantern.

"Hello?" I asked. "Anyone out here? Sam? Abby?"

I crept through the barn, heading toward the back door to check on the chicken coop. Halfway across, I stumbled and tripped. As I tumbled to the ground, the lantern slipped from my grip, rolling across the barn and extinguishing as it crashed into the wall. I was left in near-total darkness, with only a few bars of dim light filtering through the barn's slats.

I could make out loud sounds coming from the coop now: banging and scraping. The chickens were going crazy.

I slowly got to my feet, peering around for the lantern, but it was too difficult to make out in the near blackness. Instead I tiptoed toward what I hoped was the barn's back door, toward the sound of the clucking chickens. I felt the edge of the barn wall and made my way to the door.

I peered around the corner of the door and gasped.

The screen door to the coop opened with a creak, and a dark figure wearing a bulky black hoodie stood silhouetted in the dim light. *A black hoodie like Bob's*, I realized. I stared at the figure, squinting to see though the gloom, but the murky darkness made it impossible to identify the person. The chickens screamed as he or she emerged, and I could see that the person was holding two chickens by the neck. A cloud of feathers puffed out of the coop after them. The figure walked a few steps and then stopped short. He or she turned slowly, and my blood chilled.

The figure was looking *right* at me. The early morning light lit him or her from behind, making it impossible to identify the person.

The figure passed one of the chickens to the other hand and pulled something from his or her waistband.

I felt my breath catch as the item caught the orange light from the sky.

It was a long, curved blade.

The figure turned the chickens clutched in his or her hand slowly, and in the dim light I could see they were stained with blood.

I choked out a gasp. Even though I knew any case could turn deadly, I hadn't really expected to find someone *dangerous* on the farm that night. Whoever was sabotaging the farm was just spraying bacteria on a bunch of vegetables. Potentially deadly bacteria, sure. But it wasn't a *violent* act in itself.

I had to get away! I closed my fingers around the phone in my pocket, but I was too late. The figure dropped the chickens—the *dead* chickens, I thought with sickening dread—and ran toward me. I yanked my hand from my pocket and ran.

I lunged away, nearly tripping over my feet in my haste to escape. *He has a knife! And he's coming after me!*

I headed back toward the hill and the tent but quickly thought better of it. Bess and George were probably safe where they were. If this person even knew they were there, it would be a while before he or she could get to them. Instead I ran for the house.

The figure was just a few yards behind me, gaining fast. I willed my feet to go faster, my lungs to hold out. *Just get me to the house. . . .* It was maybe fifty yards away, over a plowed field of eggplant. There was no time to veer around the crops. I ran right through them. I was just a few feet from the narrow backyard when my foot got tangled in a vine and I felt myself yanked down toward the ground. The impact knocked the wind out of me, and I felt the sticky, squelchy ooze of wet mud.

BANG! BANG!

I struggled to my feet, the mud letting me go with a reluctant belch. *It couldn't be. But . . .*

BANG!

The sounds were shots. The figure was shooting at me.

CHAPTER EIGHT

Fresh Blood

I RAN LIKE MY LIFE DEPENDED ON IT . . . because it looked like it did. I scrambled out of the mud and into the grassy yard, over the short distance to the porch, up onto the porch.

BANG!

I ducked down instinctively. But nothing sailed past me; in fact, I realized I wasn't hearing the bullets make contact with anything. *Maybe he or she is just trying to scare me off,* I thought. But it was cold comfort. I kept running.

When I hit the top step, the bright-yellow porch

light went on. *It must be motion-activated.* I ran to the door and pounded on it, then turned and looked behind me, hoping that I could identify the mysterious figure in the blaze of the porch light.

But when I turned around, there was no one there. Was he or she lingering just outside the yellow beam of light? Or had they given up?

I pounded on the door again. The house was silent. I turned and looked at the yard, which was empty. *But is the attacker still out there?* My heart thumped in my chest.

I raised my hand to pound on the door again just as it opened, and suddenly Abby stood there, wearing a blue bathrobe and a confused expression. "Nancy?" she asked. "Is everything—?"

I pushed past her through the foyer and into the kitchen. "I have to come inside!"

Abby moved aside to let me in and closed the door. "Are you all right?"

I stood in the middle of the kitchen, leaned on the table, and took a deep breath. *In. Out. In. Out.* "Did you hear the shots?" I asked.

"*Shots?*" Abby asked. "What?"

As quickly as I could, I explained what had happened with the noises from the chicken coop and spotting the intruder with the knife—and then being chased and hearing the gunshots. "He or she was wearing a hoodie," I said. "A black hoodie—like Bob's."

Abby looked as stunned as if I had slapped her. "Bob?" she echoed weakly. "But—"

"Oh my God!" I cried as I suddenly realized. "Bess and George are still out there in the tent! If whoever's out there found them . . ."

Abby drew her lips into a thin line. "I'll wake up Sam," she said. "He'll fetch the hunting rifle and go get them. Try not to worry."

Try not to worry! Ha! But before I could reply, Abby was already halfway upstairs. I tried again to take deep breaths. *You're okay. Sam's going to get Bess and George. It's all okay.*

But then I jumped; I could have sworn I heard footsteps downstairs. *Is someone else up?* I crept to the door of the kitchen and peered into the foyer, but I couldn't see anything. I nervously crossed the foyer and looked into the living room. *Does Bob have a house key?* I wondered. And then I remembered the thought I'd had earlier this morning: *maybe the culprit is in the house.* Realistically, wasn't it likely that whoever I'd seen by the chicken coop had a personal reason to sabotage the farm? What was more personal than family? I stepped into the darkened living room, lit only by the early dawn light coming through a large bay window. I looked beneath the window and jerked back.

Someone's on the couch!

But closer inspection revealed that it was only Julie—lying down, asleep.

"What are you doing?"

I jumped again; a male voice, coming from the foyer. I swung around to face Jack, who stood in a pair of striped pajamas, watching me.

"How long have you been standing there?" I asked.

Jack shrugged. "A couple of minutes?" he said, moving into the living room. "Something woke me up.

I could have sworn I heard the chickens going crazy, and then—a loud bang."

"It was shots," I said, trying to catch my breath. Jack's voice had startled me. "Someone attacked the chickens in the coop. I caught them, and when they saw me, they chased me across the fields and shot a gun."

"A *gun?*" Jack asked, frowning. He crossed his arms in front of his chest. "That seems . . ."

But I'd stopped paying attention to what he was saying. My focus was drawn to the sleeve of his pajama top, which was stained with a few bright-red blobs.

Fresh blood. Whoever had killed the chickens couldn't have avoided getting some of it on his or her clothing. Maybe Bob wasn't involved at all. Maybe he was fast asleep in his bed across town, and had been all night.

Maybe I was looking at the chicken killer. And nearly *me-killer.*

". . . probably just a car backfiring, don't you think?" Jack was asking. He stepped forward, his expression cold.

I had no idea what he was talking about. *Where are Sam and Abby?* I stepped backward, willing Jack's parents to come down the stairs.

I heard movement behind me. Julie was stirring on the couch, wiggling and rising up on her elbow. "What time is it?" she asked sleepily.

"It's about five," Jack replied. "Sorry we woke you. Did you sleep any better down here?"

Julie yawned and nodded, sitting up. "My back was *killing* me in that bed," she said, stretching her arms over her head. "This couch is just hard enough to balance me out. Once this baby is born, maybe I'll sleep again."

"Oh, sure," Jack said sarcastically. "Having a newborn baby in the house is great for sleep, I hear."

There was a clattering on the stairs. Sam stomped down, dressed in a red bathrobe and holding a hunting rifle. His hair stood up in every direction. He looked right at me, concern in his eyes.

"Are you all right?" he asked.

I nodded. "But Bess and George . . ."

Sam nodded quickly and turned toward the kitchen. "I'm going to get them right now. Don't worry, Nancy. If there's someone out there, I'll find them."

He disappeared into the kitchen, and I heard the screen door slam. Abby descended the stairs, peering in at Jack, Julie, and me.

"What happened?" asked Julie, frowning as she looked from me to Jack and Abby.

Abby sighed. "Why don't we all come into the kitchen and I'll make some tea," she said. "I'm afraid there's been another . . . incident."

Abby frowned as she handed Jack his tea. "Is that blood on your sleeve?"

Jack glanced down, and his face darkened for a moment. "Oh, it is. I had a nosebleed earlier. I get them when I'm stressed. Sometimes they can be pretty . . . severe."

"Well, that must be new. I don't remember you ever getting them as a kid. But here." Abby went to the sink and wet a paper towel, then handed it to her son. "Maybe you can get some of it out."

Jack took the paper towel and scrubbed at his sleeve. "As we were saying," he said, "that's quite a story, Nancy."

I'd given an account of everything I'd seen since I'd heard the commotion in the chicken coop—leaving out a few details, of course, in case they became important later. "I'm not sure what you mean," I said, sipping my tea.

Jack shrugged. "It's just—you're saying someone brought a knife and a *gun* to harass some chickens?"

"Whoever it was, they weren't just harassing chickens," I pointed out. "They were killing them."

"Oh, right," Jack scoffed. "Because you need two weapons to kill a couple of hens."

I raised an eyebrow. "So you don't believe me?"

Abby gave him a chastising look. "Jack!"

Jack shook his head. "No, no. I didn't say that," he said. Then he turned to me, his eyes calculating. "It's just—Nancy is young. If she was scared, maybe she imagined some things she didn't really see."

I don't have time for this, I thought with irritation. "You think I made up the shots?"

"Jack!" This time his wife yelled at him. "Don't be—"

But Julie was cut off by the screen door banging open, and George and Bess piling into the kitchen in their pajamas.

"Nancy, are you okay?" Bess asked, moving to the table with wide eyes. "Sam told us . . ."

"I'm fine," I said, standing. "Are *you*?"

George nodded, stepping up to the table beside Bess. "We're fine," she said. "It sounds like we slept through all the excitement. Sam just came and woke us and explained what was going on."

Sam stood at the doorway now, rifle still in hand. He waved. "I'm going to take a look around," he called to Abby. "Just to make sure there's nothing out here."

"Be careful!" Abby called to him. "Maybe you should let the police handle it. . . ."

But Sam gave her a dismissive wave of the hand. "This is *my* farm. I can protect it." And he disappeared from the doorway. A few seconds later we heard him clambering down off the back porch.

Abby gestured for Bess and George to sit down. "Can I get you some tea?"

"Oh, that would be great, thanks," Bess said with an enthusiastic nod. George agreed too, and they both took seats.

"Nancy," said Julie gently, "are you going to sit back down?"

I realized awkwardly that I was staring. Right at the blood on Jack's sleeve. *A nosebleed?* The blood was bright red and fresh. Was he saying he'd been woken up by the chickens, got up, got a nosebleed, cleaned it up, and *then* came downstairs?

I tore my gaze away and turned to Abby. "The thing is, I have kind of a headache."

Abby turned from the stove to shoot me a sympathetic look. "Poor dear," she murmured. "The stress, probably."

"Maybe," I said. "Do you have any aspirin, or anything I could take? Maybe that would help."

Abby nodded. "Of course!" She put the kettle back down on the stove and turned to walk toward the foyer. "It's up in—"

"Oh, that's okay!" I scrambled from the table toward the foyer. "I can get it. I need to use the bathroom anyway. Where did you say it was?"

Abby gave me directions to the upstairs bathroom, and I forced myself to file them away for future reference. Jack and Julie had fallen into a quiet side conversation, and Bess and George were watching me with mild curiosity.

"Poor Nancy," Bess said in a *tsk, tsk* kind of voice. "She gets headaches all the time when she's worried. You should see her during final exams!"

Don't oversell it. I shot her a look. "I'll be right back!"

And I scampered up the stairs to the second floor, leaving everyone to their tea.

The bathroom was exactly where Abby said it would be, second door on the left. But I walked right by, peering into the other rooms. I found what I was looking for at the end of the hall. A smaller bedroom, too neat and uncluttered to be the master suite, containing two suitcases and an array of personal items. *This must be Jack and Julie's room.*

I crept into the bedroom. One of the suitcases was set up near the doorway, and I flipped idly through it, finding only maternity clothes. *Julie.* I dropped the clothing and crept farther into the room, spotting the other suitcase on the other side of the bed. I walked over to it, crouched, and began sorting through the clothes.

Button-downs and jeans. Sweaters. Socks and underwear. No black hoodies, no more bloodstains. I stood up and looking around the room. On the dresser sat a laptop computer, open. I walked over and glanced down, pleased to see a PROPERTY OF JACK HEYWORTH label with a cell phone number on the keyboard. As I tapped the keys to wake up the screen, I felt a little flash of guilt. *What if Jack isn't responsible for the sabotage?* I'd be spying on his e-mails and Internet history for no reason.

But what choice do I have?

None, I realized. Given what was at stake, I had to take a look.

Then a terrible thought occurred to me: *I don't have my memory stick.* I always carried a portable flash drive on my key chain. If I'd had it, I could have copied all the files on a computer or e-mail account onto it, then reviewed them later. But my memory stick was sitting in the tent out in the fields, along with all my other belongings.

I sighed. *I'm going to have to just look quickly and try to get through as much as I can before someone finds me up here.* Biting my lip with determination, I clicked on the e-mail program and brought up the most recently used e-mail account, whose password the computer was thankfully programmed to remember: JHeyworth@fastmail.com. I went into the sent folder and, not even bothering to open the messages, forwarded all the e-mails for the last three weeks to my own e-mail account. Then I deleted *those* messages from the sent folder so Jack wouldn't see what I'd done.

I glanced at the clock: 5:53. Had I come up here at 5:40 or 5:50? I couldn't remember. *Just keep looking; I don't hear anyone.* I clicked on the Internet browser and went right to the "history" folder. Nothing immediately jumped out as unusual . . . the *Chicago Tribune,* NPR, eBay, Google. I followed the link to Google and typed "how to" in the text bar, to see whether any recent searches came up. Nothing. Then I tried "where to get" and waited for the site to fill in the missing words. New text flashed up, and when I read it, my heart nearly stopped.

Where to get E. coli?

Jack had entered that question just two weeks before.

A chill went up my spine. *Am I sitting at the computer of the person who tried to kill me?* Maybe not. There could be a totally reasonable explanation.

Or . . .

"Nancy?"

I nearly jumped ten feet in the air at the sound of a voice from the doorway.

"What are you doing in here?"

❧

CHAPTER NINE

Caught in the Act

THE VOICE WAS JULIE'S.

Uh-oh. I struggled to push my overtired, over-worked brain into action.

"Is that Waikiki?" I asked, pointing to the photo of a smiling Julie and Jack on a beach that served as the computer's desktop. "Because it's so weird, but I could *swear* I was on that beach last year." I took a step back from the computer and gave an awkward laugh, looking around like I was just realizing I was in Jack and Julie's room. Julie watched me, a little crease of confusion forming between her eyebrows.

"I'm sorry, I know I'm being nosy," I went on. "I just spotted that photo from the hall and it brought back all these memories of this great vacation I took. . . . I think I'm a little loopy from lack of sleep!"

Julie's eyes warmed with sympathy, and she stepped into the room. "I can relate," she said with a little smile. "Actually, that's Costa Rica, not Hawaii. It's beautiful, isn't it? Jack and I took a vacation there last year and stayed in this gorgeous little eco-resort. We slept in a hut right on the beach. It was *amazing*." She sighed, looking at the photo, then shook her head. "Of course, that was before I lost my job, back when we had disposable income." She laughed a bitter little laugh.

"What?" I asked.

Julie shrugged. "Oh, I lost my job as an investment banker last year. You know—they keep saying the recession is over, but for bankers, is it really?" She smiled, like she was making a joke, but when I didn't laugh, the humor left her face. "Anyway . . . finances have been a lot tighter lately. In fact, Jack and

I originally came out here to look for houses in the area. We're thinking about selling our apartment in Chicago."

I raised my eyebrows. "You can't quite afford it anymore?" I asked, filling in the blanks.

Julie nodded, then shifted her eyes uneasily. "*And* we'll need more room for the baby," she added. "*And* it won't exactly hurt to have Jack's parents just a few minutes away. Abby's such a peach, she's offered to watch the baby a few days a week for me if and when I find a new job."

Money problems? It seemed Jack's potential motivation to destroy Black Creek Farm went even deeper than I thought.

Julie smiled brightly. "Anyway," she said, "I came upstairs to look for you because Sam just came back. He says someone vandalized the chicken coop and killed three of the chickens! Can you imagine?"

I shook my head, then caught myself. "Yes," I said. "I mean, no, I can't imagine *wanting* to do that. But it doesn't surprise me that it happened. I actually saw the person out there. . . ." I couldn't help shuddering, remembering that tense moment when the intruder had looked up and seemed to spot me peeking around the coop. *What would have happened if I hadn't been able to outrun him? Or her,* I reminded myself.

Julie was watching me with sympathetic eyes. "How horrible," she said. "I'm so glad you got back to the house safely." She paused, shaking her head. "Honestly, I can't *believe* what's been going on at the farm these past few days! I thought coming to the country would be *relaxing*. But this is more stressful than the city!"

I smiled ruefully and nodded. "Maybe you'll need to go back and, like, listen to car alarms going off for a while to relax," I suggested.

Julie laughed. I noticed then that her eyes looked tired; she must have been telling the truth when she said she hadn't been sleeping well lately. "Well, I think I'm going to take a shower," she said, gesturing to a door that opened off the rear of the room—a private bathroom, I guessed.

"Oh, of course," I said, moving toward the door to the hallway. "I'm sorry to keep you. I should get downstairs to hear the latest, anyway."

Julie smiled as she brushed past me. I paused in the doorway, watching her flip on the light and push open the door. Just as she ducked inside I saw it, thrown over a towel rod.

A black hoodie.

I had to bite my lip to keep from letting out a gasp.

CHAPTER TEN

A Clear Message

"NANCY, WHY ARE YOU DRIVING LIKE A maniac?" Bess grabbed the handle on the passenger-side ceiling of my car and gave me a horrified look as I just barely missed the bumper of an old Chevy, skirting around to pass it on the right.

It's your fault for going so slow, I thought when I saw the driver glance up in alarm, and then scolded myself. *Stop it, Nancy. Don't be the kind of driver you hate.*

"I'm sorry, Bess," I said. "I just really need to get home and talk this out with you and George."

Bess raised her eyebrows. "So you have a theory?"

"I do. And it took so long to make our report to the police and get out of Black Creek Farm, I was beginning to think I'd never get to share it with you."

Bess grinned. "Well, do tell! I always love hearing the latest deductions of Nancy Drew, Super Sleuth."

I smirked at her. "You know I can't tell you without George here"—Bess pretended to scowl—"but I can't wait to tell you guys what I'm thinking. More than anything, I want to figure out our next step!"

Bess glanced out the windshield. "Well, I'll give you this, Nancy," she said. "When you want to drive fast, you really do drive fast! We're nearly at your house already."

Minutes later I pulled into my driveway, and we piled out and ran into the house. Pausing only to grab two oatmeal raisin cookies from the cookie jar on the counter (*Thanks, Hannah!*), we hightailed it up to my room, where I pulled out my own laptop.

I pulled up the home page for my e-mail program and logged in, then opened up my in-box to start sifting through the messages I'd forwarded from Jack.

"What are you doing?" Bess asked. "Or can't you tell me that, either, till George gets here?"

I rolled my eyes at her. "No, I'll tell you. I forwarded myself a bunch of e-mails that Jack's sent in the last three weeks. I'm going through them now, looking for anything suspicious."

"Jack," Bess said simply. Her blue eyes sparkled with excitement.

I looked over at her. *Darn, did I just give away my whole theory?* "Um . . . yeah. Jack."

Bess nodded slowly, tapping her chin. "He *was* very rude at the buffet," she said. "And then with what Lori told us . . ."

I had turned my attention back to my computer screen, where suddenly something caught my eye. "Oh my gosh!"

Bess jumped up from my bed and darted over to my desk to look over my shoulder at the computer screen. "What is it?"

It was an e-mail from Jack, sent, according to the time stamp, at around four o'clock that morning.

Dude . . .

Look, what we're doing is having no effect. There's more fun planned for tonight, but I'm not sure it will work. S is too hardheaded.

We need to talk about sending a clearer message.

Maybe if S had an "accident" . . .

Meet me at Coffee Cabin in River Heights this afternoon at three.

J

I looked up at Bess. Her mouth was hanging open.

"An 'accident,'" she said slowly. Then she made finger quotes. "*'Accident,'*" she repeated.

"I know," I said.

"Do you think he's going to hurt Sam?" Bess asked.

"I don't know. But it sounds like that's on the table."

Bess looked horrified. "Three o'clock . . . what time is it now?"

I glanced at the clock on my computer screen. "It's one thirty."

Just then George breezed through my bedroom

door. "Was that you I saw driving like a woman in labor?" she asked, looking at me like I was out of my mind. "It couldn't be, right? Aren't you always telling me that just because I *can* drive the speed limit doesn't mean I *should* go that fast? What were you in such a rush for?"

I gave George a matter-of-fact look. "I think I've figured out who's behind all the shenanigans at Black Creek," I said, "and if we don't stop him . . . Sam is going to get hurt!"

CHAPTER ELEVEN

~ঙ~

Coffee Stakeout

I PEEKED OUT OF THE KITCHEN AT THE Coffee Cabin, watching the door as I adjusted the volume on the microphone I'd hidden under table four. Table four was the most popular table in the place, according to George, and very centrally located. If I was really lucky, Jack and his accomplice would take a seat there to have whatever sordid conversation they were planning to have, and I'd get a crystal-clear recording that I could bring to Sam to show him the ugly truth. If I was only a little bit lucky, they'd sit somewhere else in the Cabin, but still close enough to the mic for me to hear what they were saying.

I worried that we'd already used up our luck allowance, though—because it was *crazy* lucky that Jack had decided to meet this person in the one coffee shop in the area that employed my amazing friend George.

"It's not too busy today," George murmured, sidling up next to me in the crisp white shirt and black apron that served as her uniform. "That's lucky. It'll make 'Dude' easier to spot."

I nodded. "I already have, like, three potential 'Dudes' picked out," I whispered. "The bald guy at table one, the redhead at table eight, and the biker guy sitting at the bar."

George surveyed my candidates with interest. "The biker guy ordered a strawberry mocha dream-a-chino," she whispered back, "just in case that takes him off any kind of 'potential criminal' list."

I shot her a horrified look. "George, criminals drink all kinds of coffee drinks!"

"There's no coffee in that," George corrected me. "But there *is* a mountain of whipped cream."

I looked back at Biker Dude just in time to watch him put down his mug, revealing a huge whipped-cream mustache. I glanced at George and couldn't help giggling.

"George, did you wipe down table seven?" George's boss, Lydia, interrupted our giggle-fest. She leaned over from her desk just inside the kitchen, frowning.

"I'll get right on it," George replied, shooting me a *sorry, but she pays me* look. Lydia hadn't exactly been thrilled when we'd explained that we wanted to turn the Coffee Cabin into a recording studio. She'd nixed Bess having any part in it, so Bess had headed downtown to get her much-craved manicure—but not before we promised to keep her updated via text. Meanwhile, Lydia had been staring daggers at my back since I'd arrived, sarcastically asking how our "little detective game" was going.

When George left to wipe the table, I looked to the doorway as the bell jingled, indicating a new customer.

When an older woman walked in, I felt myself deflate a little.

I looked out the window, across the street, where a River Heights police cruiser idled. I'd had quite a hard time getting the River Heights Police Department to take me seriously when I'd gone into the station to tell them everything I knew about the Black Creek case. They told me the only crimes actually committed (the vandalism and contamination of the crops) had been outside their jurisdiction, and that a meeting of two potential culprits didn't warrant sending an officer to the scene. It took a gentle reminder that the noted attorney Carson Drew would be *very upset* if anything were to happen to his darling daughter to get them to agree to send Officer Bailey over to wait outside the café in his squad car, "monitoring the situation." He still looked pretty unhappy about it, with his folded arms and grim expression. He glanced over at the coffee shop, and I waved brightly. I swear he rolled his eyes before giving an exaggerated yawn.

I was so busy watching Officer Bailey that I almost

missed the door opening again, setting off the jingling bells. George was nearly back to the kitchen and turned to look too. When I saw who was entering, though, I frowned. It was Holly, George's old Girl Scouts leader. If she saw us here, she'd want to know what was going on with the Black Creek Farm case, and I didn't want to get into a long conversation with her that would distract me from Jack and "Dude." I ducked into the kitchen just before Holly could spot me and waved to George to wait on her. George nodded and walked out to the register.

"Can I help you?" I heard.

"Omigod, *George*! I totally forgot you worked here! Can I get a large soy latte?"

"Of course! How are things going?"

"Oh, you know, I can't complain. I just started teaching this new yoga class over at the community center—water yoga? Have you heard anything . . ."

I tuned their voices out and turned back to the door.

A familiar car was pulling up outside. *Jack's.* I felt my stomach drop.

The driver's-side door opened, and a figure climbed out. When the door closed again, revealing the driver, I let out a gasp.

It wasn't Jack—it was *Julie*!

Julie was "J"?!

My jaw dropped as I quickly ran through all the evidence in my head. The motivation, needing money, wanting Black Creek Farm to fail so there would be a larger inheritance if anything happened to Sam. *Check.* Julie would benefit from a larger inheritance just as much as Jack. And the computer I'd taken the e-mails from—it could have easily been Julie's e-mail account, couldn't it? And the black hoodie on the towel rack . . . *it could have been hers!*

The only strange thing was that Julie was the one who'd gotten food poisoning at the buffet, setting this whole terrible string of events in motion. *Or did she?* I thought, and my heart thumped. It was a stroke of genius, in a way—Julie's getting food poisoning while pregnant was more dramatic and scary than anyone else who could have gotten sick. But would a pregnant woman really knowingly poison herself? Was Julie so desperate that she would endanger the life of her unborn chid?

Then I remembered the night before—when I'd been chased by the figure at the chicken coop. Julie had been sleeping on the couch. *Or had she?* I just assumed she'd been there all night when I stumbled upon her sleeping on the couch. But I'd gone into the living room in the first place because I'd heard someone moving around, someone I'd later assumed was Jack. But wasn't it possible that Julie was sneaking back onto the couch after sneaking back into the house?

My heart was racing now, the way it does when I've just about solved a case. But I forced myself to take a breath. I knew I wasn't done. I needed Julie to meet with whomever she was meeting with, and have whatever conversation she planned to have, and get it recorded, before I could talk to Sam about next steps.

Who would believe a pregnant woman poisoned herself and then killed a bunch of chickens, anyway? It sounded ridiculous.

Julie walked purposefully toward the Coffee Cabin, then suddenly stopped and looked around. She walked over to one of the few sidewalk tables and sat down. I gulped; the weather was chilly today, and I'd never considered that "J" and "Dude" might like to sit outside. Our only microphone was inside at table four. And while it had a pretty good range, there was no way it would pick up a conversation from the table where Julie was sitting outside.

Someone has to move the microphone!

But who? It wasn't like I could casually stroll outside and stick something under Julie's table without her noticing. I looked desperately at George. *She's my only hope.* As if sensing my stare, George turned around and looked at me, and I made a crazy, hysterical sort of gesture that I hoped translated to *Come here right now. Please, please, please, I need you!!*

George raised an eyebrow, turned to Holly, and cleared her throat. "That sounds amazing," she said warmly, "but can you excuse me for a minute? My boss is calling me."

Holly nodded and smiled as she took her latte, and George walked back into the kitchen. "What?" she demanded.

"You have to move the microphone," I said, pointing urgently out the window. "See? They're sitting outside."

George looked to where I was pointing, then shot me a stunned look. "Julie?" she asked.

"Right," I replied. "Looks like I had the wrong *J* person all along."

George sighed. "Okay, but how do I move the mic?" she asked. "It's not exactly a normal motion for me to slip something under a table."

"It's more normal for you than for me," I pointed out. George looked skeptical. "Listen, just take it with you when you bring the menus, and find some excuse to bend down. Drop something, whatever."

"You make it sound so easy," George muttered.

I grabbed her shoulder, looking at her pleadingly. *"Please, please, please, please . . ."*

George shook me off. "Okay, okay. I'll try."

I watched her walk out into the dining area and carefully untape the mic from under table four. Then, with a final look back at me, she grabbed a few menus, opened the front door, and walked over to the table where Julie was sitting.

My heart was pounding as George handed Julie a menu, then purposely dropped it on the ground, knocking over the sugar dish in the process. What looked like a hundred little pink and white packets scattered over the terrace, and I watched George shake her head and gesture wildly for Julie *not* to help. Finally Julie seemed to settle in her seat, and George picked up the sugar and, pretending to duck back down for one more packet, carefully stuck the mic to the underside of the table.

I let out my breath. *Oh, thank you, George.* I was still going to be able to record whatever Julie said—and stop her before she could hurt Sam.

I pulled out my tablet and put on my headphones, adjusting the mic's sensitivity and volume.

". . . didn't know you worked here," Julie was saying to George.

George laughed. "Oh, it's kind of a new job for me. But I'm getting really good at making little designs in the foam of a cappuccino, so I'm learning marketable skills."

Julie took a second to laugh, but when she did, it was a hearty laugh. "Oh, I just discovered this new baby store in downtown River Heights," she said. "Have you heard of it? It's called Rattle and Roll."

George shook her head. "No, but I'm not really in the baby-stuff market," she said with a smile. "Did you buy lots of fun things?"

Julie's smile faltered, and I remembered what she'd said about their money problems. "Just a few," she said more quietly. "Can I have a minute to sit with the menu before I decide?"

"Of course. I'll be back in a few."

George walked back inside, shooting me a questioning look. I gave her a thumbs-up.

But just then, someone from inside the café bumped into George on the way out. *Holly!*

"Is your latte okay?" George asked.

Holly looked at her, almost seeming surprised to see George standing there. "Oh . . . oh *yes*! It's great. I'm just heading out to meet a friend."

George smiled and nodded, and Holly continued outside.

Her friend is here? But there was no one outside but . . .

Julie.

Holly sat down across from her, and Julie leaned over to hug her.

I felt my heart thump in my chest. *Is it possible?*

J = Julie, and Dude = . . . *Holly?*

CHAPTER TWELVE

~❧~

Things Fall Apart

IT MAKES SENSE, I THOUGHT WARILY. IN Julie's current state, she would have needed an accomplice. *Holly contaminated the food at the buffet after she and Lori had washed it and after Julie ate. Either Julie or Holly or some combination vandalized the greenhouse, and Julie attacked the chickens and shot at me last night. Then she snuck back onto the couch just in time for me to find her there.*

I couldn't imagine why Holly had joined forces with Julie. She seemed so supportive of Black Creek Farm, and so gung ho about local, organic, sustainable food in general. *Why would she help destroy a farm that's such a great example of all the things she supposedly stands for?* I didn't know, but I intended to find out.

Julie leaned over to Holly. She was whispering, but with some quick adjustments to the microphone controls, I could still hear her.

"There's a problem," she was saying, peering inside the dining room. *"That girl."* She jabbed her finger in George's direction. "She's been at the farm with her friends—including that little detective girl Sam met the night of the buffet. I don't think for a minute that someone her age could outsmart us, but I don't really feel comfortable talking turkey with her so close."

Holly followed her eyes, nodding. "Maybe we should go somewhere else," she whispered. "George is pretty smart."

Julie stood up from the table. "We'll drive somewhere," she said. "Find a Starbucks or something. I could actually really go for a Frappuccino. . . ."

My stomach sank. If Holly and Julie left, all of

George's hard work reattaching the mic to the outside table would be for naught, and my plan would be shot. Again. There was no way I could follow them and inconspicuously plant a microphone at a new location, which meant I wouldn't get the full story. Not to mention there was no way Officer Bailey would follow, especially if Julie and Holly went to another town. I'd have to kiss good-bye to the idea of a recording that could stop Julie from hurting Sam.

There was only one thing I could do. And it scared me senseless.

"George!" I hissed at my friend, who was busing some tables in the corner. She looked up and walked over.

"You know," she said, "some people raise a hand in the air and say, 'Excuse me, miss.'"

"I'm not trying to order a cappuccino," I said, pulling off my headphones and handing them to George. "I need you to listen for a minute."

George frowned. "Okay, but no more than a *minute*. Because Nancy, you know if I'm gone any longer,

Lydia will freak. She's probably ready to kill me over this whole thing already."

We turned back and looked at Lydia. She was wearing headphones of her own and staring at her laptop screen. When she saw us looking, she made a wild gesture for George to get back to the dining room.

"One minute!" George called in a weirdly high voice, holding up one finger. "You have *one minute*, Nancy."

"That's all I need."

I burst out of the kitchen before I could lose my nerve and walked straight through the dining room and over to Julie and Holly's table outside.

"Hi Julie. Hi, Holly," I said loudly. "I think we need to talk." I lowered my voice. "You know what about."

Both of them turned to me. Julie's expression turned murderous when she realized who I was. "What are you doing here?" she asked with a sneer.

"I think you know," I said, willing myself to stay calm. "The thing is, Julie, I managed to get a photo of you on my phone last night. Blown up on the computer, the photo is clear—it's pretty easy to identify you."

Julie turned pale. I looked over at the squad car, hoping to catch Officer Bailey's attention.

Except the squad car was empty. *What the . . . ?*

"Is that so?" Julie smiled at me, a sickly sweet grin that made my stomach do a flip. She leaned closer. "That's very interesting, Nancy, I'm not going to lie. I think you should get into my car so we can go somewhere and discuss this further."

I snorted. "You think I'm going to get into a car with you?" I asked. "Do I look that crazy?"

Julie leaned back and folded her arms on the table. "No," she said, "but I think you love your father that much."

My *father*? "What does this have to do with my dad?" I asked.

Julie tilted her head. "You've probably guessed this already, since you're such an *ace detective*," she said in a sarcastic tone, "but Jack is working with us." She glanced at Holly. Holly's mouth dropped open, but her expression gave nothing away. "He has the gun I used outside the chicken coop last night. I had a feeling you might be a problem for me today, so Jack is currently sitting in a rental car outside your house, just waiting for the call from me," she said. She held out her hand, pistol-style, and mimicked shooting. "Bang, bang! Is your dad home today, Nancy?"

He was. In fact, I'd said good-bye to him less than an hour before.

"I don't believe you," I said quietly.

Julie smiled again, a cold smile. "How *much* do you not believe me?" she asked, pulling a phone from her purse. "Enough to stake your father's life on it?"

I lost my breath. *No*—and Julie knew it.

Without thinking, I turned and looked into the café to see if George was watching. She was—in fact, she'd moved out of the kitchen and was standing just inside the dining room, headphones on, holding the tablet. She was looking at me like I'd lost my mind.

"Your friend had better come too." Julie's voice was low, threatening. "I know she's in on this with you."

I turned back to her to see that she'd seen me look at George. And worse, Holly was glancing between us nervously. I saw something in her eyes that looked like genuine fear. "If either one of you screams, I'll make that call to Jack. I'm sure he could make a visit to George's house too. Understand?"

I swallowed hard and gazed desperately at the squad car. It was still empty. George stepped out of the café, and I squinted past her into the dining room, hoping to see Lydia watching—but she must have still been in the kitchen/office. I looked at George, trying to put all the *I'm so sorry I looked back* I was feeling into my frantic expression. We were about to get into a car with a total maniac, and nobody would know. *How did this all go so wrong?*

Julie stood, and Holly slowly got to her feet too. "You're going to walk calmly to the car," Julie said, "like nothing is wrong."

George looked at me, her eyes glassy with fear, and gave a slight nod, as if to say, *Let's do what they say.* She left the tablet and headphones inside the café and met us outside. Together, we walked slowly to Jack and Julie's gray sedan. Julie followed, smiling like we were all going on a picnic, and unlocked the doors, encouraging us all to "Climb in—don't be shy!"

George and I settled ourselves in the backseat. Julie and Holly slammed the doors, and there was a loud *click* as they locked. I reached instantly for the handle on the inside of the door, but it wouldn't budge; *Child locks*, I mouthed to George. We couldn't unlock the doors and get out—even if we were willing to escape a moving car. We had to go wherever Julie wanted to take us.

I glanced out the window just in time to spot Officer Bailey leading two teenage boys out of an alley down the street. I recognized the teens as Toby Farelly and Steve Minerva, two boys who were known throughout River Heights to have a rather colorful history with the law. Each of them was holding two cans of spray paint. *Of course,* I realized; Officer Bailey must have seen an actual crime being committed and decided to go after the vandals. It only made sense, since he hadn't exactly been excited to be keeping an eye on me to begin with.

I tried the door handle one more time, then the electric windows, but neither worked. Finally I gave up and just pounded on the window.

"*Officer Bailey!*" I screamed as loud as I possibly could. "Help us! She's kidnapping us! *Officer Bailey!*"

Our car peeled out of its space just as a hand smacked me hard across the face. I blinked and looked up front; Holly had hit me. Julie had both hands on the wheel.

"You'll pay for that," Julie said darkly, anger seeming to emanate from her body.

I didn't doubt that I would. But I had only one chance to get Officer Bailey's attention.

I looked back at him. He was watching our car speed off.

Did he see me?

CHAPTER THIRTEEN

Into the Woods

"WHAT DO WE DO WITH THEM?" HOLLY asked hesitantly. She shot a nervous glance at the backseat, where George and I were watching them curiously.

"What do you think we do with them?" Julie spat. "They know everything, Holly. We can't just drop them off at their parents' houses."

"Maybe . . . ," Holly said slowly. "Maybe we could take them somewhere and lock them up? My grandparents have a summer cottage I don't think is being used right now. It's about an hour away, but . . ."

"That's not enough, Holly." Julie's voice was as

sharp as a knife. "They can't be out there, knowing what they know."

I looked at George in alarm. *They're going to kill us.*

She looked at me and said nothing, but a tear escaped from her left eye.

I felt like my heart might explode. To keep sane, I decided to do the only thing I knew how to do in this situation: get the criminal talking.

"What exactly happened, Julie?" I asked in as gentle a voice as I could manage. "I mean, there must be a reason you did what you did."

Julie let out a rueful laugh. "Oh, there was a reason," she said. "I lost my job last year, as you know. It was a very lucrative, high-paying job. Losing it was a pretty huge blow. Jack's a lawyer, sure, but half the cases he works are pro bono. We burned through our savings really fast. We started having trouble paying the mortgage on our apartment. We couldn't afford the payments on our cars and had to give one up." She paused. "Meanwhile," she said, "my wealthy father-in-law—who, back in the day, had more money than Jack or I could shake a stick at—helped one sick girl's family and decided to pursue this cockamamie organic farm idea, sinking half his net worth into it. Did I mention that Sam had left Jack half his estate in his will? Jack and I watched our inheritance dwindle for more than a year. Then I got pregnant, and I decided I had to do something about the farm."

George cleared her throat. I could tell she was scared. "But isn't this kind of . . . extreme?" she asked. "I mean, if your ultimate goal is just to get him to sell the farm. Now you're kidnapping us? Maybe . . ."

Hurting us, I finished for her. But George's voice was gone. She couldn't say it.

"It wasn't meant to go this far," Julie said with a sigh. "I mean, the farm was already struggling. I thought Sam would only need one really disastrous year to realize what a big mistake he'd made. Hence, the contaminate-the-vegetables-with-E. coli plan. I wasn't exactly thrilled about the idea of giving myself E-coli. But I had my family to think about. I figured once word got around that Black Creek Farm was selling vegetables that could actually *make you sick*, that would do it. But the thing is"—Julie let out a crazy laugh—"Sam didn't give up."

"He loves the farm," I said, wanting to keep her arguing with me.

"He does," said Julie. "And he kept fighting, and got you and your friends involved. I realized the stakes had to get higher, faster. I knew that Sam was a softie. I knew he wouldn't put up with danger to his family."

She suddenly pulled into a parking lot. I looked around. *Kepner Park*. It was a large park just outside River Heights that had a small pond and hiking trails.

"Anyway," Julie said, turning back to face us with that same deranged smile, "now we're going to go for a hike."

I looked at George. *She wants to get us out into the woods and do something to us,* I realized. *Maybe something so horrible that we'll never come out.*

George looked like she had reached this conclusion as well.

"Come on." Lifting her phone and giving it a little

shake, Julie herded us out of the car and onto the blue hiking trail. I looked around at the parking lot, heart pounding, wondering if this was the last piece of civilization I'd see. But then Julie shoved me along.

"Let's go."

We walked down the trail for maybe half a mile. Then Julie stopped us. "Into the woods," she commanded. I felt my stomach clench. *This is bad. This is really bad.* But for once my mind was blank. I didn't know what else to do.

George and I followed Julie's commands and left the trail, walking farther until we reached a small clearing.

"What are you going to do to us?" George demanded.

Julie smiled, pulling a long, sharp-looking knife from her purse. There was still red on the blade. Julie looked at it and laughed.

"Sorry, girls—there may still be some chicken blood on there," she said.

I felt like I was going to be sick. I reached into my pocket, trying to dial my dad on the phone without being detected. *Do I even have service?* I couldn't tell if my fingers were hitting the right buttons.

Julie moved closer to me and held up the knife, her hands shaking. "You're first," she said, "since you're the sneaky one."

I felt like I was in a nightmare; I wanted to scream or run, but my feet were rooted to the spot.

Julie held the knife high. It gleamed in the sun.

"No!" Holly's voice suddenly split the air. "Julie, don't!"

Julie turned and glared at her accomplice. "What's your problem now?"

"It's not worth this," Holly said, and as she moved closer, I could see that her face was ghostly white. "Listen, I'm passionate about this CSA and the principles it stands for. So when I agreed to contaminate those vegetables at the buffet, I only did it because you're my best friend and you were desperate. But you swore no one would get hurt. And I'm not okay with hurting people, Julie, especially not *kids*." She gestured helplessly at George and me.

Julie stepped closer to Holly and held out the knife. "Holly," she said in a cool voice, "if I'm willing to get rid of two teenagers over this, why would you assume I'm not willing to get rid of *you*?"

I gasped. Had our last hope of making Julie see reason been defeated?

But then I heard the slightest bit of movement.

I turned toward the trees we'd walked through to enter the clearing and spotted Officer Bailey, creeping forward with a gun trained on Julie. I took in a breath, but he held his finger to his lips and I forced myself to look away.

"FREEZE! Drop your weapon!"

Julie turned around, startled, to face Officer Bailey and three of his finest colleagues, all with guns trained on her.

Relief washed over me like a hot bath on a cold day. *He did see me*, I realized with satisfaction. The ruckus I'd made just before Julie raced out of her parking space had worked.

Julie struggled, but eventually the police forced her

to drop her weapon. I was beginning to realize that Julie was seriously out of her mind; clearly, the woman had no idea when to give up. When the knife was down, I nearly collapsed with relief. I ran to George and hugged her as hard as I could.

"Please forgive me," I cried. "Please, please, please, please, please, George . . ."

"Forgive you for what?" she asked, pulling back with an expression of genuine confusion.

"For looking back at you in the café," I said, thinking it was obvious. "If I hadn't done that, they might not have made you get into the car with me."

George shook her head. "Nancy, they saw me earlier. I waited on them."

"But—"

"Shhhh," she said, hugging me hard again. "I would have done the same thing. And honestly? I'm just glad we're alive to tell the tale."

Once Julie and Holly had been handcuffed and led out to the police cruiser, Officer Bailey came back to lead George and me back to the parking lot. Just as we got there, a familiar car squealed into the parking lot, stopping short. The door flung open, and my dad came running out toward us.

He grabbed me in a big hug, then pulled back and looked us both over. "Are you girls okay?" he asked. "Nancy, what on earth are you doing working a case this dangerous without my help?"

I shrugged, not sure what to say. "It didn't seem that dangerous at the beginning," I said honestly. "I mean . . . who knew people could get this worked up about organic farming?"

CHAPTER FOURTEEN

~♌~

Harvest Time

"OOH, IT'S REALLY GETTING CHILLY," SAID Bess, pulling her wool cardigan tighter around her as we moved through the buffet line in the outdoor tent. "The growing season's almost over."

"And thanks to Nancy," Abby said with a smile as she spooned some eggplant curry onto our plates, "Black Creek Farm has had a very successful year after all."

We were back at Black Creek a few months after all the excitement. Sam had invited George, Bess, Ned, and me for an end-of-harvest dinner and celebration.

The farm looked incredibly beautiful, covered in all its fall foliage. Pumpkins were growing in half the fields now, and Abby said they were having great luck selling them at the farm stand and at local farmers' markets.

"How is Jack doing?" I asked Abby.

"He's right behind you," she said with a wink. "You can ask him yourself."

I turned around and found—sure enough—a tired-looking but cheerful Jack, holding a baby boy in a carrier.

"Nancy!" he greeted me. "Have you met Owen?"

"This is Owen?" I asked, leaning in and gently touching the baby's tiny curled-up fist.

Jack nodded, smiling. "He *almost* slept six hours straight last night."

I laughed. "Is that good or bad?"

"It's good!" Jack said. "For his age? It's very, very good. But anyway, thank goodness for my parents. If they weren't here, if they hadn't offered to let us move in, I don't know what I'd be doing."

After the dust had settled in the case against Julie, it had become clear that Julie had been lying about Jack sitting outside my house with the gun. Jack really hadn't known anything about her plan to convince Sam to close Black Creek Farm. Julie had the baby shortly after being placed in custody and was still in jail, awaiting trial, along with Holly. Things didn't look good for Julie, but Abby had told me that Jack still brought baby Owen to visit her every other week. Their marriage was over, but Jack wanted Owen to know his mother.

"I'm so glad it's working out for you," I said honestly. "You look—happy!"

Jack smiled. "You know what? I *am* happy," he said. "This isn't how I pictured this happening at *all*, but the whole experience has brought me a lot closer to my family. And it's made me realize—all the silly, petty things I was worried about before Owen was born? Complaining about my inheritance, which Julie clearly took a lot more seriously than I thought? None of that matters. The more I learn about the farm, the more I like it. I'm just enjoying getting to live here with my parents."

"It sounds like you've really come around to Black Creek," I said, smiling.

"I have," Jack admitted. "It's a great place. And I'm excited for this little guy to grow up here."

Just then I spotted someone I really wanted to see out of the corner of my eye. I asked Jack if he could excuse me, put my plate down on a table, and ran over.

"Sam!"

The gray-haired, rosy-cheeked farmer turned and faced me with a big smile. "Nancy! I'm so glad you and your friends could come."

"How are you feeling?" I asked.

"I'm *great*," said Sam. "Not completely cured. But it looks like the first round of chemo is working, and my doctors seem optimistic."

"That's fantastic!" I cried.

"It is!" Sam agreed. "Plus, the farm is thriving. I mean, look at all the people here. This is only about half of our CSA members. It's weird, but the publicity we got from the whole Julie debacle has really driven a lot of customers our way. We're breaking even for this year, and if this continues, it looks like we'll do much better next year."

"I'm really happy for you," I said sincerely. I'd grown fond of Sam in the short time we'd worked together. It was great to see how his life had turned around in just a few short months.

"Well, we have you to thank, Nancy," Sam said, patting my shoulder. "Meeting you at that buffet was the best thing that could have happened to me. I'll never be able to thank you enough for what you've done for our family."

I shrugged. "Give me a hug, and we'll be square."

So he did—and we were.

I went back to pick up my plate and move through the rest of the buffet. Then I joined George, Bess, and Ned at a small table at the edge of the tent. They had already dug into their dinner, which they all agreed was delicious. I took a bite and let out a little sigh of pleasure.

"This tastes amazing," I said.

George smiled. "So, Nancy," she said with a mischievous look, "has working on this case made you want to get more involved in the growing of your food?"

I poked a carrot with my fork. "Actually," I admitted, "I think I'm done with farms for a while—though I *did* sign my family up for the Black Creek CSA next year!"

Dear Diary,

THOUGH IT'S FAR FROM AN IDEAL SITUA- tion, I'm happy that Jack is making the most of it at Black Creek Farm. And who knows—maybe little Owen will grow up to follow in his grandfather's footsteps? I'm just relieved that Sam can continue to follow his dream, with his family supporting him every step of the way.

And luckily for my dad and me, Hannah has already started planning healthy menus around our Black Creek Farm CSA share. For now, though, I have to run—Ned's picking me up for a decidedly _un_organic burger-and-fries date.

READ WHAT HAPPENS IN THE NEXT MYSTERY

IN THE NANCY DREW DIARIES,

A Script for Danger

Dear Diary,

A FEW MONTHS AGO, THE *RIVER HEIGHTS* *Tribune* announced that Alex Burgess, an exciting new director, was shooting a film in River Heights—starring Brian Newsome! Since then, everyone has been buzzing about how exciting it is to have one of Hollywood's biggest stars in our little Midwestern town (especially Bess, of course).

I've always thought it would be thrilling to visit a movie set—the actors, the costumes, and watching a story come to life. I never imagined that most of the drama would be behind the camera...

Action on the Set

"I THINK I'M GOING TO FAINT."

Bess Marvin, my best friend, lifted up her sunglasses and surveyed the scene in front of us. It was nine a.m. and we had just arrived at the River Heights train station, which was filled with giant trucks, trailers, and a few dozen spectators, all waiting as anxiously as we were.

"He's just a person!" snorted George Fayne, my *other* best friend and Bess's cousin. Although she and Bess are related, they are complete opposites. Take their outfits this morning: Bess was dressed in an elegant blue wrap dress with intricate embroidery along the neckline. Her hair curled softly around her face, and she was wearing just the right amount of mascara to make her lashes look "natural but flirty," according to her. George, on the other hand, was not pleased about getting up so early, and could barely be bothered to throw on a pair of cutoff jean shorts and a faded T-shirt that had been through one too many spin cycles.

"Ned texted me to say that he saved us a good spot," I said, shepherding my friends through the small but eager crowd in the parking lot. Many people were holding signs that read BRIAN, I LOVE YOU! and RIVER HEIGHTS WELCOMES BRIAN NEWSOME!

Although I wasn't as star-struck as Bess, I certainly felt like this was a special moment—a real film crew was about to start shooting a movie in River Heights. The director, Alex Burgess, had worked in my dad's law office before pursuing his dream of directing films. Neither my dad nor I were surprised when Alex made the move to Los Angeles. Although he had been a diligent paralegal, he'd always been obsessed with movies.

Alex had struggled at first, working in a diner while writing the screenplay for his film, *The Hamilton Inn*. His sacrifices had paid off though, and now here he was, ready to bring his story to the silver screen.

But it wasn't Alex the crowd had come to see; it was the star of his film, Brian Newsome, who played a handsome doctor on the hit television drama *Hospital Tales*. As my friends and I made our way through the shrieking fans, I noticed that many of the girls in the crowd were dressed as nicely as Bess was.

"Nancy! Over here!"

My boyfriend, Ned Nickerson, stood at the front of the crowd with a camera around his neck; he free-lances as a part-time photographer for the *River Heights Tribune*.

Bess barely said hello to Ned, craning her neck toward the side of the parking lot. "Have you seen him yet?"

Ned smiled. "Brian should be here in about fifteen minutes, Bess."

I caught George rolling her eyes and grinned. George usually has little patience for Bess's celebrity crushes.

"Nancy, I cannot believe you know the director of an actual movie! This is so cool!" Bess continued.

I nodded, adding, "It's really generous of Alex to invite us here to see the set!"

George yawned. "Why is the coffee cart closed?" she grumbled. Besides not being a morning person, she also hated being hungry. The combination of the two had turned her into a full-on grouch.

"Several businesses in and around the train station had to shut down for the day to accommodate the shoot," I explained, "so Alex wanted to do something special for the business owners and employees to thank them. Especially because he's from River Heights."

"So they lose a whole day of business and all they have to show for it is a photograph with some fake doctor?" George snorted.

"Um, *Hospital Tales* is one of the most watched

shows on television," Bess snapped, "and Brian Newsome happens to be an amazing actor, *Georgia*."

Everyone knows that the best way to ruffle George's feathers is to call her by her real name, but I jumped in before George could unleash a snarky comeback. "The movie is paying all the businesses too," I said. "And Alex invited a few old River Heights friends to come to today's photo op, like my father and me. He thinks it will be helpful to have familiar faces here."

"We're lucky," Ned agreed, looking up from his camera. "I've heard that most movie sets are closed to the public because of issues with security and sound and—"

"Psycho fans?" George smirked, elbowing Bess, who ignored her.

"They're going to ask everyone to leave the set before they start shooting," I announced.

"Leave where?" Bess asked hopefully. "Where does the set end?"

"Technically 'the set' refers to the area that will be on camera," Ned replied, "but I'm guessing they'll clear out the whole train station and the parking lot because it's filled with their trucks and trailers. Sorry, Bess."

"So what's this movie about, anyway?" George asked, yawning again.

"All I know is what I read in the *Tribune*," I said. "It's a mystery about a brother and sister who move back to their hometown to run their family's old, run-down hotel . . . which might be haunted."

Bess added, "Brian Newsome will be playing Dylan Hamilton, and Zoë French is going to be playing his sister, Malika. Zoe's done some television as well as theater and commercials, but *The Hollywood Times* thinks that *The Hamilton Inn* could be her big break."

"I guess those are for the actors, then." I pointed toward the parking lot entrance, where three long, white trailers were lined up. One of the trailers had two doors labeled "Dylan" and "Malika." The door to an especially tall trailer was cracked open slightly, and I could see racks of clothes lining the walls. I figured that was the costume trailer.

It was impressive, really: the vehicles, the bright lights, the crew members wheeling crates and trunks of equipment around, the tangle of wires running all over the ground.

"Wow," I said. "Making a movie is a lot more complicated than pointing a camera and yelling, 'action!'"

"No kidding," George muttered. "I just wonder how they *feed* all the actors."

Ned grinned. "There are pots of coffee and pastries, George." He pointed to a table covered in breakfast goodies that was set up near the entrance to the train station.

"For *us*?" George's eyes widened with joy.

"That's what I heard!" Ned laughed. "Plus, isn't that Mayor Scarlett chowing down on a bagel over there? She isn't part of the crew."

"If you say so, Ned!" George trotted off happily.

I smiled at Bess. We both knew that the best way to improve George's mood was by promising free food.

As George waited in line for breakfast, I noticed a fortysomething woman in a wide-brimmed straw hat and brightly colored floral pants speaking angrily to Mayor Scarlett. I toyed with the idea of trying to get closer to hear what she was saying when something bumped softly into the side of my head.

"Oops, sorry," a voice apologized.

I turned to see a pale girl in her early twenties holding a metal pole with a professional-looking video camera attached to the top of it. I could barely see her features underneath her heavy dark-rimmed glasses. A lone wisp of her chestnut brown hair was visible from underneath a white baseball cap.

I suddenly recognized the girl's face. "Cora? Cora Burgess? Is that you?" I asked.

She nodded, eyeing me suspiciously.

"I'm Nancy Drew, Carson Drew's daughter. Alex used to work for my dad." I stuck out my hand.

She raised her eyebrows in recognition. "Oh, right. Hi, Nancy." After a few seconds of awkward silence, she took my hand in a feeble shake. Cora was Alex's younger sister, and I'd met her a few times when she visited her brother in my dad's office. As

I remembered, she hadn't been terribly friendly back then either.

Just then, George returned with a cinnamon roll in one hand and a croissant in the other. "You guys should get over there if you want some. All the good stuff is going fast," she announced.

"No thanks," Cora replied, looking disgusted. "That food has been sitting out since, like, six a.m."

"Hey, if I remember, it was *your* dream to go to film school, Cora," I said, changing the subject.

Cora nodded slowly. "Yeah, I'm in my second year. I'm doing a behind-the-scenes documentary about Alex's movie this summer."

"Wow, that's amazing!" Bess exclaimed, clearly impressed. Before I could introduce my friends, Cora said, "Excuse me, I have to get back to it. Nice to see you, Nancy." She disappeared into the crowd.

"You'd think she'd be more excited about being behind the scenes on a real film set," George remarked. Flaky bits of croissant fell onto her shirt, and she brushed them off.

"Well, it was *her* dream to be a filmmaker." I shrugged. "Maybe she's jealous that her brother just changed careers," I snapped my fingers, "and is already directing a movie of his own."

Ned smiled and patted my shoulder affectionately. "That's our Nancy," he chuckled. "Always looking for motives, even when there's no mystery."